LOVE
&
PEACE

LOVE
&
PEACE

ABHISHEK KOTHARI

Srishti
PUBLISHERS & DISTRIBUTORS

SRISHTI PUBLISHERS & DISTRIBUTORS
Registered Office: N-16, C.R. Park
New Delhi – 110 019
Corporate Office: 212A, Peacock Lane
Shahpur Jat, New Delhi – 110 049
editorial@srishtipublishers.com

First published by
Srishti Publishers & Distributors in 2017

10 9 8 7 6 5 4 3 2 1

This is a work of fiction. The characters, places, organisations and events described in this book are either a work of the author's imagination or have been used fictitiously. Any resemblance to people, living or dead, places, events, communities or organisations is purely coincidental.

The author asserts the moral right to be identified as the author of this work.

On 19 September 2006 I saw a girl. All I remember about that meeting is – she was wearing a white top and wore lip gloss. In time, we became very good friends. Though I never liked her hands, I wanted to hold them forever. Ha, I had fallen in love with her! And on 21 November 2006, I proposed to her. She rejected me. Of course it hurt! In time, our friendship also flickered. We stopped meeting. In fact, we stopped talking. My friends told me that I did not deserve her love! However, with a dream that one day she'd love me back, I moved on. I didn't stop loving her. I simply waited for our time to come. Meanwhile, I made her sketches and portraits. I developed a habit of writing songs and letters for her, which I never sent to her. Thinking she'll be moved, I wrote my first novel A Feeling Beyond Words to show her what love is to me – to show her what she is to me!

On 9 August 2010, when my first book was launched, she met me at my house.

"Look, I am already in a relationship with someone. He loves me, and I love him too. His family has accepted me, and my family knows him well. It's final. I am his," she said. I am his! That killed me. Right then. Right there. It struck deep inside my heart. My heart and lungs almost jumped out of my throat. I sat there numb, looking at her. I had no words to say, or justify myself. I showed her a portrait I had made of her. But she was not convinced. She was not moved. How could she be? She herself was in love with someone else. So she left. That was the first and the last day that she visited my house – a place I had dreamed for her to rule being my Queen.

I didn't meet her after that rainy day. I didn't even talk to her. Days turned into weeks, weeks into months, months into years. And as you read this, it's been more than six years now, and we're still *out of touch. But news travel, you know. This November 2016, she got married to the one she told me about on that rainy day. Of course, once again, it hurts. Still, I can't stop loving her. I have tried, but I have failed.*

I dedicate this book to you, Aparna, wishing for Love & Peace for you, always. I don't believe that if we're not together, or couldn't be, means I can't love you. I believe that some feelings are embraced, others are not, but what matters the most is the passion and honesty with which we love. I love you! Though unrequited, I have managed to love you for a decade, now I am trying to love you for a century.

Acknowledgements

$\mathcal{I}$ would like to acknowledge and express my gratitude to *you*, dear Reader-Friend, for picking up this book.

I am indebted to team of Srishti Publishers for believing in me once again, and their valuable inputs in the book.

With deepest gratitude, I would like to thank Sumit and Urvashi, for holding me when every other person stepped back.

For their generosity in love and support: Shailender bhaiya and Shivani bhabhi.

My friends with whom I have developed an everlasting bond: Aman, Mrs Bakshi Bhawna, Deepesh, Gaurav Bagaria, Jui, Kanu, Kushagra, Nikhil and Raghavi.

Every good thing needs an inspiration. For me, you have done the cause! I thank you, the very special Sonu Purohit, for being my backbone to finally come up with this book, from discussing the characters to writing a concept, for saving me from falling apart when I felt a part of me dying...for everything. I *really* feel blessed that we met!

And finally to *love*, that gives me a reason to breathe and write. I feel, the day love leave me, I will leave this beautiful world.

To know more about me and the book, do write to me at writerabhishekkothari@yahoo.com.

A note from the author

This is life. People come and go once their purpose is solved. But then there are a few those reside in our hearts beyond eternity. When life is harsh and all seems falling apart, they come for our rescue like angels. They hold our hand, support us, inspire us and make life heaven. For me, you have done that!

I had my reasons and issues in settling down, so a few years ago, I left home to travel the world, explore the undiscovered, and pen down my feelings. Then, somewhere in the middle of the journey, it happened – we met. You radiated the supreme positivity and I was just mesmerized by the simplicity in you. And once I met you, I felt like putting an end to the journey, for I felt it was complete. That you are the destination. Then once I knew you, we came closer. I made up my mind that a new journey has to begin.

You know, My Fairy in White, when I looked into your eyes, I could see the purpose of my life – you – for, if asked, you are the one I regard the most. You're the one who has given life a reason and the one who makes me happy. I feel complete when you are close.

So, dear Pagli, here I declare to feel honored and blessed that we met and I feel proud to express that I love you – truly, madly, deeply – with all my true feelings!

With planning and hard work, we can win anything; but love, as it is spontaneous, won me unalarmed. Now that I love you and dream of making you My Lady in Red, I love you unconditionally and without any hesitation. I vow to love you, encourage you, trust you, and respect you. As a family, we all shall create a home filled with learning, laughter and compassion. I give you my word to work with you to foster and cherish a relationship of equality, knowing together we all shall build a life far better than any of us could imagine alone. You are my eternal love. I accept you as you are and I, you know, am already yours. I will care for you, Queen of My Heart, stand beside you, and share with you all of life's adversities and all of its joys always, till our life sees its evening. The same day, I shall take my last breaths in your arms. Meanwhile, let's love, live and forgive.

Prologue

"What is love?"

"Love is what I earn in order to move further every day. It's the source of feeding my soul to live a day longer, in order to continue my journey and pursue my dream – that is you. For me, love is you."

"Why do you love me so much, Raju?"

"Why don't you love me so much, Guddi? Forget so much. Simply why don't you?"

"That's not the answer."

"Still. Answer me first."

"Simply…I simply don't," she answered.

"I do," he smiled. "I simply do."

She sat silent. He added, "I love you so much because this is how I am, and because this is the only way I know of loving, in which I breathe to take a step further to reach out on to you, and to show you my love by all means, so purely that when you smile, a curve comes on my lips, and when you are in pain, my heart bursts out and wishes to destroy the entire world. Above all, loving you this much gives me peace."

Late twentieth century

"Your first love is the perfect and only love, until you meet your second love," his lady love had said years ago, and then had married someone else.

Sanjay sat on a log lying on ground. As he looked at the sky above, he saw birds flying back to their nests; the red sun at the horizon bidding goodbye for the day; and the moon smiling in the sky to welcome everyone into his world.

'I never thought I'd return to such matters,' he thought. To love deeply in one direction makes us more loving in all others. Unable to contain his sympathy, he broke all the promises he had once made to himself and came back to the matters of the heart – to help someone in love.

"Pranam, Bhaiji," a voice greeted Sanjay.

Sanjay turned his head to find Harish and Madhav standing behind him. Bringing his hands together into a namaste, Harish bowed, the tip of his forefingers touching his nose. Sanjay stood and dusted his pants. He did not reciprocate Harish's namaste with words. However, he nodded casually and holding his pyjamas with his left, he put his right hand into it. Harish and Madhav grinned at each other, wondering what Sanjay was trying to do.

"Who is the boy?" asked Sanjay. Thankfully, his hand was out now.

"Don't know, Bhaiji. Someone from Birogi gaon," replied Harish, terrified to see the pistol Sanjay had taken out from his pyjamas. He looked around to check if anyone was there.

"Sit!" Sanjay ordered Madhav to sit on the crossbar of his bicycle.

Harish looked at Sanjay. "Do you need a special invitation?" Sanjay frowned. "Back on the carrier." He gestured through his eyes.

Everybody was afraid of Sanjay in the village, so the friends obediently did as commanded. They didn't even ask where!

A lady emerged from a nearby farm. She was wearing a sari, her face covered with a dupatta. She held a sheaf on her head and, with a piece of cloth, had a sickle tied on her waist.

"Madhav!" she screamed seeing the trio approaching. Unable to see her covered face, Madhav tried to recognize her from her voice, but failed. Sanjay didn't stop and they passed her. As Sanjay peddled the bicycle, she turned and screamed, "What has happened to Raju?"

"Why do women need to know everything? Always looking for gossip!" muttered Sanjay.

They crossed a small temple. Harish and Madhav bowed their heads. They wished someone would put some sense into Sanjay's head. Seeing both friends bowing their heads, Sanjay clicked his tongue for he had stopped believing in god years ago. Harish pinched Madhav from the back.

"Ouch," screamed Madhav, and then stopped in between, as he realized he had almost sent an invitation to Yama's messenger who was halfway to meet him.

"These girls will never learn. Every disastrous thing happens because of them. The world's longest battle – the battle of Troy, India's biggest battle – the Mahabharata. Even our brother…he has turned insane. It's all because of women," he said with bitterness.

Madhav observed that Sanjay had a lot of bitterness for women and that he wanted to vent the whole of his spleen on Guddi and her lover.

Sanjay had taken them to a jungle outside the village. It was dusk; it was silent all around. Sanjay was drunk and the other two were afraid of the dark, ghosts, wild animals, and of what Sanjay was up to. Having reached a spot, the two friends saw a few men sitting in a circle, consuming local liquor.

"Hello, sir," Sanjay said from a distance to one of the men as he stopped peddling and rested a foot on the ground.

A gigantic man stood up and approached the trio. Madhav and Harish got down from the bicycle. Sanjay parked the bicycle on its stand and hugged the man. He introduced Sanjay to the other men. Madhav and Harish stood silent maintaining their distance.

"Younger bro quarreled with someone and he raised his hands on my bro. He dared to raise his hand on my bro!" Sanjay lied.

"What! How come?" asked the gigantic man.

"They're juvenile. Things like this happen at this age," Sanjay paused, and looked at the other men from the corner of his eye, and asked, "Assassinate?"

The gigantic man sighed. "Up to you."

"You tell."

"Tomorrow morning," the big guy said reluctantly.

"Right now!" Sanjay was persistent.

"Then shoot."

"One more thing."

"What?" the huge man asked as he finished his peg.

"Abduct a girl as well?" Sanjay added casually.

"Girl?"

"Yes, I'll give you an account later."

"Okay. Do whatever you want to, but keep me informed. I'll handle the matter," said the gigantic guy. Others were listening, without saying anything. Sanjay met all of them, swallowed one peg at once, and came to Madhav and Harish. Unable to respond, and terrified by the proceedings, the two friends were speechless spectators, wondering who the hell these men were.

"We'll abduct the girl first, ask her the boy's house, and then I'll shoot the boy. Okay?" Sanjay confirmed, while he checked bullets in his pistol. They went back towards their village on the bicycle.

'Abduct Guddi? Kill her boyfriend?' thought Madhav and Harish.

"Where does she live?" asked Sanjay.

"Don't know," lied a petrified Madhav and Harish, clearing their throats.

It was late. Darkness had descended and they had just crossed the temple again. Both friends, Madhav and Harish, thought of the consequences if someone caught them. Heavy charges would be applied and the next day, the news would spread all around the village – two boys and a young man were caught with a loaded pistol. Promises, pledges, assurances, oaths were used to convince Sanjay to go home, but nothing worked.

"Bhaiji, if you don't mind, may I ask you something?" Madhav managed to utter.

Sanjay nodded, but kept riding.

"You're doing all this because I told you Raju got mad because of one girl? Moreover, since you too were in love once, you don't want our friend to go through all that pain you have endured, right?"

Though in a very respectable tone, Madhav managed to continue. He was gathering his courage as he felt it was his duty to ask Sanjay why he pitied the madman he hardly knew. Love had taken Sanjay from away his family years ago, and today it was taking away their friend away from them. The two of them, who had left home at dawn, stopped by a waterfall to hear Sanjay.

"Nonsense," replied Sanjay, with bloodshot eyes. He was panting. From his bulging eyes seemed to spurt inner violence of an uncontrolled nature his body could hardly contain.

Sanjay continued, "Do we think of our parents when we fall in love? We fall in love when we have to and we must, and when we fall in love, we give our own life to them. In love, we belong to them, but they never belong to us. And when some time passes and we become mature, we think exactly as a mature person does. We change. We too fall in love, but there are so many other things as well – parties, career, illusions along with our parents, whose call we would have answered. Now at our age, the love for our partners is still great, and stronger than the love for our parents."

There was a silence all around. Sanjay seemed to be filled with emotions. Though he was saying one thing, his heart was screaming something else.

"Shouldn't we consider the feelings of our lovers? Isn't it natural that they consider the love for their hearts greater than anything in life? Parents exist, and they are the only reason of your existence on this earth, your only god, to whom each of us must pray. We must defend them. And when our love changes, they don't want tears for us, because when we cry, their soul cries. Now, if one lives safe and happy, without having hurt anyone, one should be happy. What more can we ask for? You should laugh, because before leaving they sent you a message that they were leaving satisfied with the most memorable memories spent and remembering you forever in their hearts. That's why, as you see, I'm not mourning. I never did, for she married her father's choice," Sanjay finished.

Madhav and Harish continued to look at him in distress.

"Absolutely correct, Bhaiji. I totally agree with you. There is no remedy for love, but more love. But what did you do? Changed yourself to prove her wrong," said Madhav. "Are you right in doing that? You were doing something to force someone, someone you loved, to curse herself throughout her life and punish her. Is it right? Have you ever been right, even for a single second, in the past nine years, Bhaiji?" Madhav broke the silence he had maintained for long.

Sanjay, thinking and drinking, had for the last nine years tried to find something to console him in his deep sorrow. His grief had been greater on seeing that nobody could share his feelings. But now the words of Madhav almost stunned him.

"We can only learn to love by loving, not by cursing or hating," continued Madhav. "A very great person has said it so well: 'Darkness cannot drive out darkness, only light can do it. Hate cannot drive out hate, only love can do that.' Love her for a reason you hate her for, and if you can't, you don't deserve to love her. Love is blind. How could you see that she was wrong?" asked Madhav.

Sanjay suddenly realized that it wasn't just the others who were wrong and could not understand him, but he himself could not rise up to be the lover willing to bid farewell without crying, not only to the departure of their love, but even to their sweet and painful memories.

"I didn't see it," said Sanjay, still trying to defend himself partially. "I felt it."

It seemed to Sanjay that he had stumbled into a world he had never dreamt of, a world so far unknown to him, and he was so pleased to hear Madhav showing him the truth. He was a tough man from the outside, but that didn't mean he was a man of no heart. He was a lover once, after all.

Then suddenly, just as if Harish had heard nothing of what had been said and almost as if waking from a dream, he turned to Sanjay, asking him, "I'm sure you loved her very much. Has your love really left you? Have you really never cried in nine years, even once after she left? Did you really spend nine years of your life doing nothing except thinking of her?"

Madhav stared at Harish. Sanjay also turned to look at him, fixing his great bulging horribly watery light gray eyes deep in his face. He tried to answer, but words failed him. He looked and looked and looked at him, almost as if only then, at that silly, incongruous question, he had suddenly realized at last that it had been nine years that his love left him forever and since then he had been doing nothing, but drinking in her memory.

He snatched a leaf in haste, and to the amazement of Madhav and Harish, broke into uncontrollable sobs.

"Please Bhaiji, don't take your anger out on anyone," Harish placed his hand on Sanjay's shoulder, carefully. "The girl you loved is responsible for your state and not the girl our friend Raju loves. Your abduction or killing someone will not help anyone. In fact, it will create panic for everyone in the village. It's good that you want to help someone in love, someone who's not fine, but what's the difference between him and you...that his condition is more severe, or yours is less? If you really want to help someone, help yourself first," cried Madhav.

"Raju needs care more than any action. And you need peace more than love," Harish joined Madhav. They both were crying by now, their cheeks flooded with tears. Both friends had cried for the first time in front of each other, and that too for Raju. They all hugged each other and sobbed.

A few days ago, Raju was found numb in his house. When he gathered himself, he cried miserably. He was lost. No thirst. No hunger. No senses. Later, he hid silently in the cattle shed and after that, his condition only worsened.

He would go and sleep in the kitchen. He would puke all over. He would pee everywhere in his room. Sometimes he would hide under a quilt and sometimes in the water tank. He would scream out loud, sometimes breaking the silence, sometimes breaking his heart. Something had certainly happened to him.

Villagers began talking about him. Deserter soldier Puri said a bad spirit had entered into him, and advised Baba to show him to the Tantrik at a nearby village. The news had reached Guddi's house as well. Her mother advised his family to show him to a doctor. A new neighbour said that instead of wasting money and effort, he should be admitted to one of the mental asylums. Those who were on their deathbeds themselves pronounced that his time had come and his soul should surrender itself to the almighty.

But Raju's family didn't cease trying. His grandmother asked his grandfather to prepare for a sacrificial ladle to control his stars. His grandfather did so, and his family did all they had been advised to do by people. From tantriks to the best of doctors in and around the district, Baba took him everywhere. But even then, there was no improvement.

What had happened to Raju, everyone wanted to know. He was the only one who knew the secret, but he was in no condition to tell anyone! To others, he had become a madman.

Sanjay, like Raju's family, had no plans of giving up on Raju. After that horrifying night, Sanjay would meet Madhav and Harish every evening, but they never showed any interest. All they said was that Raju needed care more than any action. Sanjay sensed what was in the heart of the two friends – fear. They didn't want anything to happen to anyone, especially to Guddi. Raju would have died had he known that Guddi had been abducted. It was enough for him to endure what had happened. So Sanjay decided to do what he had decided a few days ago.

After a lot of research and advice from his friends and contacts, Sanjay found out a way. He advised Baba to take Raju to Lucknow's renowned psychiatrist, Dr M.S. Mishra.

"Don't worry, Uncle. I'll take care of the expenses. Dr Mishra is a family friend. After all, your son is my younger brother," said Sanjay.

Raju was taken to Lucknow. On Dr Mishra's advice, Raju was admitted to the mental institution – The Home. After completing all the formalities and getting Raju admitted, Baba and Sanjay went to meet Dr Mishra before leaving for Dhaneri.

"Okay sir, entrusting our life in your hands, we're leaving today. Kindly do whatever you can to make him better," said a tensed Baba, joining his hands.

Dr Mishra understood Baba's helplessness and clasping Baba's hands, assured him that Raju would be taken good care of.

"Why do you worry when you have an elder son like him?" said the doctor. He exchanged a smile in sympathy with Sanjay who was standing behind Baba. Sanjay smiled back.

"Have faith in us. We'll give you good news soon," the doctor said and proceeded towards his chair. Baba turned to leave along with Sanjay.

No sooner did they reach the doorstep, the doctor's voice stopped them. "I forgot this."

He took out a poly bag and kept it on his table. "Your son had this with him."

Sanjay collected the packet and once again, after joining his hands into a namaste, he left.

Sanjay and Baba went to the bus stand. The heat in Lucknow was at its peak. Their clothes were dusty and sweaty. The dust, noise and crowd further added to their misery.

"Did you check what is in the packet the doctor gave you?" asked Baba.

Hawkers who had been selling fruits, orange-shaped candies and ayurvedic powders started getting down when the bus conductor started pushing them off.

"No," said Sanjay. He took out the yellow coloured poly bag from his bag. The bus began to move and soon the conductor started distributing tickets. Sanjay took out a bundle from the yellow poly bag. It was a bundle of loose sheets tied gently with a ribbon. He opened the knot and held the first page in his hand. Baba peeped into it.

"Do you remember this?" Sanjay asked Baba, giving him the page.

Baba's heart turned heavy. "I had written this letter to him a year after his mother left us."

Sanjay took the letter from Baba and read it. He checked the bundle and found that it had more letters, from Guddi this time, and notes written by Raju. Educated people often call them journals. In a hope to find the mystery of Raju's madness, Sanjay started reading the sheets.

The first sheet read:

One should never defame love because
it is the purest of all feelings.

Love is the best ever thing that happens to one.

Love sagas are more than true; not because they tell us that life exists, but because they tell us that life exists only to love and be loved.

I believe in love and its beauty. For life teaches a lot, whereas love brings utter transformation in an individual, and makes him a master.

I believe that the power and depth of love should be known to everyone — that love lies somewhere deep inside the heart, that love is spontaneous and eternal, that love should be beyond limits, that love is virtuous, that love is one essential element of everyone's life, and that life is meaningless without this element.

Love is a gift. I believe, everyone, to a certain degree, should experience it, though very few possess it. An experience sometimes can be painful, but love — it is always ecstatic.

Love is such a beautiful thing, and there's so much to do.

However...

Love forces one to take unpredicted risks. When it is in excess, it brings a man neither honour, nor worthiness.

With that, Sanjay turned the pages of the journal and lost himself in Raju's world.

Tears in my eyes remind me of Maa. I know it is not the correct way to start something with tears, but I am helpless. Moreover, tears are all I have with me right now. There are two people I have loved the most – Maa and Guddi. None of them are with me. Maa left me a year back, and I left Guddi a year back, just after a few days of Maa leaving me.

After that I came here to Kanpur to work with Hoshiyaarji. He is a good man, a Sikh. He owns a shop here in Kanpur. When people like me travel alone, far away from their houses, and they have no idea where to go and what to do, then people like Sardarji are the ones who come to the rescue. When I had come to Kanpur from my village, I was not aware of life away from home. It was Sardarji who gave me food and shelter. He allowed me to stay at his godown behind his shop. Then, one day, I offered to wash his scooter, and got a permanent job. I became his servant. From washing his scooter to taking care of the godown and the shop, I did everything for Sardarji. He is a good man and has always paid me well. I started sending a major part of the money earned back home, keeping little for me. Sundays were off, yet I worked. I learnt a bit of lala-giri from him. And in a year's time, I had started working full-time in his shop. I had almost forgotten my old life.

But a letter from Baba this afternoon brought back memories… something I had been trying hard to get over. I know why I am being called.

Quick trip, in and out. I am from Dhaneri, a very small village in the Banda district of Uttar Pradesh. My father is a farmer, and though I was born in a Thakur family, money is something I didn't get to see since childhood. Born into a poor family of a backward village, I had grown amidst cow and buffalo dung, kutcha houses, kutcha roads, child marriage, domestic violence, superstition, black magic, and one of the biggest fears – the fear of god. Whenever anyone was in any problem, the village priest never missed an opportunity to fill his own house with at least two months of ration. I'm sure, he still does! When I was a child, I had fancied of becoming a priest, seeing everyone bowing in front of him, even the landlords. But that feeling ended as I grew.

I was sent to the only so-called school in my village. The school was just a room, with no chairs, no tables, no fans, no electricity, and most of the time, no water too. During summers, students would sit inside the class, and during winters in the sun outside that unfurnished room. There was only one teacher in the school for all the twenty-five students. The teacher was okay. He knew addition and subtraction! And also knew a few words in Hindi. But he hardly showed up, for most of the times one of his buffalos was pregnant.

Students didn't have their own books, and all twenty-five students of different classes used to sit and study together. Still, irrespective of education and environment, my parents wanted me to touch the sky. I was a sincere student. I gave my best. Not because I had to touch the sky. I knew that was impossible. I gave my best to impress Guddi.

My village was crappy, which it still is, just like my country; and crap was my school, which it still is, like my country. But it has given me two good things – friends Harish and Madhav, and could-have-been-wife Guddi. My friends Madhav and Harish had become victims of child marriage when they joined school.

Just imagine, marriage before the first day at school. But I often wondered why I wasn't married when others were. One day Madhav and Harish asked me when I was getting married.

"Soon," I replied.

And then they would keep asking me when and to whom? The asked when? Soon, I said. With whom? Guddi, I said. I did not love her. I felt insignificant beside married Madhav and Harish. It was a wish of getting married to someone, just because my friends were married, and Guddi was the only girl I knew, so I became her suitor.

Years passed, and finally I decided to ask Maa about it. Every child was getting married, so why not me. Guddi is unmarried too, Maa, I thought I'd tell her. Maybe she'd get a hint. So, one day, gathering a lot of courage, I went to Maa.

"Maa..."

She was taking out flour to make chapatis. "Hmm."

"When did you get married?" I managed to ask.

She continued to mix flour. "I think I need more water," she murmured.

"Hmm," I said.

"Pass me some water," she said.

So I did. "Yes, what were you saying?" she asked.

But the validity of my courage ended with her uninteresting mood. "Will you teach me to cook?" I ended up saying.

She was delighted. Why? I wondered at times. Maybe she wanted company. But I saw an opportunity to get close to her and talk to her about my marriage. Every morning I would wake up and study. After studying I would go and help Maa make our food and, after having brunch, I would leave for school. In the evening I would return and over dinner, I would have conversations with Maa about my life and career. I always felt confident sharing my dreams with her. My dream of getting married had brought Maa and me close. But I couldn't gather enough courage to talk to her about my marriage. In a hope that one day I will surely talk to her, I kept nurturing our relation. Every night, having shared my dreams with her, I would study some more after our long chat and then sleep on the floor.

During that learning phase of my life, Maa gave me a guru mantra. "Beta, you are growing up. And with age, a man's desires also grow. Of these desires there are some which he achieves, and the remaining ones, he dies trying to achieve. In every man's life a time comes, sometimes more than once, when he is faced with failure. Most men break during those challenging times. When my son's time comes, I don't want him to break. And if you do, then collect the scattered pieces and join them. Try again to accomplish your dream, until you achieve it. The best way to achieve the greatest of your dreams is to continue to move on and never stop, until your breath stops. With this attitude, you can win the world," she had said.

I learnt a lot from Maa during those times, and lived by those mantras always. When Maa says something, you should listen, and you should obey.

Yesterday I asked my mother why wedding dresses are red in colour. She said, 'Red signifies love and shows the guests that your bride will love you a lot.' And then I double-checked it with my father. Guess what his answer was?" asked Harish.

"How would I know?" Madhav replied, giving him an irritated look.

"My father gulped a peg, looked at me, and said, 'The sky is blue, and grass is green; there had to be something red also, or not? Else, where will red go? Plus, it's an indication to the bride's in-laws that a witch has come to suck their blood.' What color is blood?"

"Red!" giggled Madhav.

We all laughed.

There's a lot to be said for self-delusion when it comes to matters of the heart. I was in Grade twelve. We were heading to school and Madhav and Harish had decided to bunk school to smoke beedis that day, but only after accompanying me and Guddi to school.

Now there was a little part I missed in schoolhood. As Guddi was always with us, I had to maintain my composure and not do anything dumb. I always laughed if she did. And not if she didn't.

"Your mother was correct, Harish; your father was just kidding," I opposed, even though I wanted to join them and laugh.

"Then why do men die before their wives?" asked Madhav.

"They want to," quipped Harish.

I didn't know what they both were up to that day.

"Hey," I said to Madhav and Harish, "why aren't you people coming to school, man? Drop your idea of trying smoking and come to school."

"We are," said Madhav.

"Yes, we are. When did we say we aren't coming to school?" Madhav and Harish hi-fived. "But not to class!"

"You can also join them if you want," prodded Guddi to me.

"No," I said.

"Why?" asked Madhav.

"Because he wants to study and score well, and when he'll score well, he'll get a shield from our principal," Harish taunted.

"Oooh," hooted Guddi.

"You two are stupid." I turned to Guddi. "Guddi, well, do you know what marriage is all about?"

Harish and Madhav looked at each other.

"Yes," she said, "marriage is a three-ring circus: engagement ring, wedding ring, and suffering." She laughed full-heartedly. Madhav and Harish joined her.

Harish agreed, "Absolutely correct. If there were no marriages, men would go through life thinking they had no faults at all."

"Yes, and you know what?" Madhav joined Harish. "In the beginning, god created the earth and rested. Then he created man and rested. Then he created woman. Since then, neither he nor man has rested."

Not to be outdone, and more than a little pissed at her companions, Guddi said, "You've got two hundred and six bones in your body. Want some more?" She made a face. "Make as much fun as you like, I'll top this year and then will laugh when the principal honours me in front of the entire school."

Harish looked at Madhav. He said, "That stupid principal has not even given a pencil to anyone. To hell with an award!"

Madhav laughed holding his stomach.

"Madhav and Harish, the fact that no one understands you, doesn't mean you're an artist," I joined Guddi.

Madhav and Harish were making fun of women, and Guddi was getting miffed. Though I was a man, and still am, I had to take Guddi's side.

"Okay, tell me one difference between a battery and a woman?" Harish smiled. I shook my head.

"At least a woman is loyal," said Guddi, looking at me. I nodded.

"And at least a battery has a positive side," countered Harish. I smiled, but hid it from Guddi.

Guddi picked up a stick and ran after Harish.

"Leave him alone, Guddi! You'll get hurt. He's crazy."

I was afraid for her, watching her chase Harish over the hilly terrain, where there is always a chance of falling and getting hurt.

"I am not crazy. I have just been in a very bad mood for eighteen years," Harish screamed from a distance.

"Okay, listen everybody, I have a question," Madhav said as Harish and Guddi rejoined the group. "A newly married man goes to his father and tells him that his wife is exactly like his mother. Guess what the father says?" he asked Guddi.

Harish interrupted, "So what do you want, sympathy?"

"I've heard that one before," Guddi stuck out her tongue at them.

Glancing at me, Madhav said to Guddi, "Tell me one thing."

I looked at Madhav in suspicion, his eyes were mischievous.

"When you get married, where do you want your husband to take you for your first wedding anniversary?" Madhav asked Guddi, a question of my interest.

I looked in the sky and sighed out of relief. I was all ears to Guddi's words.

"I have no plans to marry," said Guddi.

I looked at her, stunned and puzzled.

"Still, if you did," persisted Madhav.

"I'd like to go to Kashmir, Goa, or Switzerland," she replied.

"And twenty-fifth?" I asked, softly, serious. I looked down. I was too scared to look at her in the eyes.

Harish jumped in once again. "On their first anniversary her husband will take her to Switzerland, because it's farthest, and on their twenty-fifth anniversary he will go back to get her. One year is enough to bear one woman, bro," he said, laughing at his own joke.

In that one moment I realised that while a mother takes twenty years to make her son intelligent, a girl doesn't even need complete twenty seconds to make him feel stupid. However, that day I realized that Guddi had not yet known the power of marriage. For her, marriage was a topic of humour. I really have to talk to Maa. If Maa talks to Guddi's parents, we'll get married soon, I thought.

Madhav and Harish were caught that day. They had left home for school, but did not reach school. They told their families that they were with me at my house, and were saved from a sound beating.

I was called back home by Baba during lunch break. All the villagers had gathered when I returned from school. Must be a kind of feast, I thought. Unknowingly, lancing the crowd at the outside, I entered the courtyard of my tiny house. I saw a figure lying on the ground, covered in a white sheet. My close ones sat on the circumference, crying, and the women howling at times. My eyes searched for Baba, but I couldn't see him. Then someone came from behind me and hugged me tight. The embrace was so tight that it bordered on suffocating. I didn't resist. I surrendered easily. Soon, I felt my back being rubbed. I wondered what was happening to me. Getting out of the embrace, I found my Nani Maa in tears. I tried to surrender completely, but she didn't hug me again.

I responded to a voice by turning back. A woman who lived five houses away from us was shrieking, *"Acha hua, joh hua acha hua!"*

I still didn't know what had happened. In very slow motion, taking one step at a time, as steadily as I could, I approached the figure.

My dream-sharing sessions, helping in the kitchen sessions, and plans of marrying Guddi – everything was dead. Maa was dead. She was lying in front of me, devoid of breath. Her eyes were closed and someone had inserted cotton into her nostrils. I wanted to scream, but couldn't. I wanted to cry, but couldn't. I wanted to shiver, but couldn't. My body didn't respond to Maa lying in front of me like that. My eyes looked for someone from the family, with whom I could at least shed tears and could ask what had happened, but I couldn't see anyone.

Holding my head, I sat there, expressionless. I stood up when someone patted my back; I was acting on reflex and followed the men.

Maa was brought to a river bank for the last rituals. When we reached there, a few people were building a platform for funeral fire. Once the pyre was done, Maa was laid on it. A few other men added more sticks to cover Maa. The priest asked me to add a few sticks as well. I did as I was told. My eyes had turned heavy by now, so had my heart. Next, I was handed a flaming stick. The priest started chanting his mantras. It was his profession, but I had never faced such a situation. He asked me to walk around Maa and light the pyre. My eyes had become moist by now. How could I do it! The priest looked at Baba, who came to me and placed his hand on mine. And then, all of a sudden, I broke into uncontrollable sobs.

I ignited the pyre with fire, and my Maa with it. And to ignite my Maa with fire, I ignited my soul with fire that day. Standing there, numb, a thousand thoughts crossed my mind.

Is this life? You struggle to live, something hits you unawares and your breath stops, and you are burnt to ashes. What after that? People mourn, or pretend to, for a while. Then they struggle with their lives, waiting for their time to turn into ashes. It's an endless cycle.

My heart died with Maa. Our relatives left after a few days, the neighboring ladies who would turn up to give Nani company in the evenings stopped showing up, and Baba resumed his farming. Things started getting back on track, except for me. I had developed a habit of visiting the river bank where I had burnt Maa, and at times I spent hours thinking of the life we had shared, dreams we had seen, and the future I had wished. I felt hurt and frustrated to have lost her.

She died, I survived. And because I survived, I died every day. Yet I breathed, for Guddi. But she had not come to meet me, or even ask if I was okay. It hurt. Neither could I live with this, nor could I change her mind about me. Those broken dreams I had shared with Maa haunted me. The air of my village turned poisonous. It choked me. My breathing became suffocating. There is always some madness in love. And also there is always some reason in madness. I couldn't bear that madness, and I used to burn from inside vigorously, so I ran away – far away from the feelings and her shadow, away from the poisonous air of Dhaneri.

I came to Kanpur and started working with Sardarji. It has been a year now, and still, I have not gathered courage to ask Baba the truth behind Maa's death. Why did she leave us? She was the only one I shared everything with. But I want to keep things the way they are. She is not with me and will never be.

Journal

It was my mother's barsi, and I had to attend it. By now, if you're reading this journal with interest, you know that I did not want to return to Dhaneri. But Baba's letter made me consider it. And after sharing my grief with Sardarji, I decided I should go home.

"You should surely visit your place and perform the rituals," said Sardarji.

He gave me a month's salary in advance and, patting my back, he added, "There'll be a difference in you when you'll return. Now go, my son."

On the day of the barsi, I was sitting in prayer with the priest and my family members when the priest said to me, "I hope you did remember the instructions I gave you last year."

He smiled mischievously, and added, "Look, it's a tradition our ancestors have been following for ages and we should continue. It's a kind of respect we owe to the dead one."

He kept lighting the diyas and continued telling me the rituals to be followed.

Respect we owe to the dead one, I thought. And how would they know we are paying our respect once they are dead. Firstly we follow all the rituals so that their soul gets purpose and it doesn't become a ghost, and later we continue following the rituals to show them respect, when neither they nor their souls exist anymore.

When man realized the importance of the words 'attachment' and 'loss', he mourned. For a time he mourned, and did not eat properly, liked solitude, did not attend functions, and did not feel festive. He was not happy. That man was a wise man. When others saw him, as foolish commoners they were, they copied him. The word 'feeling' was unknown to them. Yet they pretended to mourn. But everyone pretended for a different duration and in different ways. So a committee came up with a rule book of practice-of-mourning. It stated:

"On losing someone close, you have to mourn. When in mourning, you have to avoid delicious food, exotic drinks, good clothes, parties, festivals, and stay away from others. When in mourning, you also have to smile less and this practice has to be followed for one year. Mourning is mandatory. Mourning is a tradition."

When? How many years ago was this introduced? In which AD? BC? Foolish commoners don't know that till date. They are blindly following it because they were forced to do so by a generation prior. Not just following, they are forcing the same onto the next generation too.

Now, in my country, in my religion, in my caste, when a close one dies, we are instructed by the priest and elders to do a few things: not use oil to cook for a year, not to wear good clothes, not celebrate any festival for a year, not consume alcohol for a year, and in short – not be happy for a year. And not because, as the priest said to me, to show respect to the one who is dead, but because, as a matter of fact, you are afraid of facing some disaster if you don't follow the rituals.

I have a different concept: instead of following the fake rituals once someone is dead, love them and respect them when they are alive.

These rituals are not meant for someone close, in fact for someone we love. I tell you, take an example of a lover. If they don't possess their love, they, like tradition, don't feel happy for a year. In fact, many a times, it takes many years for one to get over a loved one. And then eating oily food, wearing fashionable clothes, celebrating a festival, or consuming alcohol doesn't come from the inside. We don't feel the urge to celebrate anything, because the heart cries. When we lose a loved one, be it family, a friend or even an animal, someone we have developed a bond with, we tend to mourn when they leave us. It's not about a year or a month, it's about a time we tend to take to get over a loss.

For me, Maa's loss was something I could never get over. Rituals for me are bullshit! Having consumed a peg of whisky to give company to Sardarji, to show him respect, or having burst a cracker on Diwali to make Sardarji's five-year-old son smile, or having eaten a poori Sardarji's wife had sent could never judge my love for Maa. Or respect, for that matter. If not outside, inside I know, I will always mourn for her, something that is natural for a son to feel for a mother he loved the most. And traditions – haaa! Sati practice and child marriage have been banned, following the prohibition of many more outdated life-sucking traditional practices that are followed blindly in this country.

Madhav and Harish had also come to Maa's barsi. Once the prayers and other rituals were over, I served them food. They insisted on eating with me in the end and they served the others with me. Pooris and kheer were served, and it did not seem as if Maa had died a year ago, but as if it was her first birthday and the guests had been invited for a feast.

Having blenched in atonement, once the bhukkar guests had left, Baba served us food. Madhav, Harish and I sat cross-legged on the floor, for our turn.

"Did you see her, man?" Harish asked in astonishment.

"Who?" asked Madhav as he tore a poori.

"Guddi," replied Harish, his eyes wide.

"Who Guddi?" Madhav asked again chewing.

"His could-have-been-wife, Guddi." Harish said pointing towards me.

My hand stopped midway as I was about to put a spoonful of halwa into my mouth. My mouth was still open, I froze.

"No," an excited Madhav said. I came into a de-freeze mode and ate my halwa.

"She was here for a while. I saw her. She took the keys from her mother and left." Harish added, "Must have come for the keys."

I learnt from the conversations that Guddi was studying arts at some degree college in a nearby city. When I left the village for my atonement, she had left the village for graduation and now lived in a hostel. She visited her parents on weekends or vacations and every time she visited, she was a topic of gossip for villagers for her clothes and changed lifestyle. Few even said she had started to see herself as a heroine and showed no respect to elders in the village when she happened to pass someone.

Harish and Madhav knew that for me, everything had ended a year ago, so they didn't say anything, nor did I. They left soon after.

But there was something inexpressible in that one moment when I had heard her name after a year. A flower gets air, sunlight, and water after a drought and a desiccated flower becomes ebullient with new life. The flower that blooms in adversity is the rarest and the most beautiful of all. This flower had turned beautiful. This flower was happy. I was smiling. And I smiled after a long time. Now this flower was waiting for butterflies and black beetles to play around. And in that waiting was an urge.

I wanted to see how she had changed. When people talk about your could-have-been-wife, it becomes imperative to go and see her for yourself. I had no plans to talk to her, go out on a date, or propose to her. The only thing that was tantalizing me now was a desire for one look at Guddi. There was a big urge to see her. Just once!

I sat on the half-destroyed roof of my house. It had been a week since the rituals for Maa's barsi, and I had plans to leave for Kanpur in a day or two. Baba and my grandparents wanted me to stay longer, but I lied that Sardarji would get angry. They accepted my plans reluctantly.

A week passed sitting on my roof, expecting a glimpse of Guddi, but I didn't see her. Guessing she had left for her hostel, I gathered the needed information from Madhav and Harish and reached Guddi's college. I looked for her at the college entrance. It was afternoon when I finally spotted her.

I always thought an artist gets attracted towards beauty, be it artificial beauty like the Taj Mahal and the Eiffel Tower, or natural beauty like snow, or the moon, or love. I had thought that the reason was probably the many relationships that artists have, and the several marriages many of them have. But that day I realized I was wrong, because I was not an artist, and yet I felt the same. I couldn't imagine that a common person could be so beautiful. I had just seen the most beautiful woman in my life. I stood at Guddi's college campus looking at her. She was not to be compared to any actress or model. Her beauty reflected of itself. Yes, she had turned beautiful!

Everybody's eyes were focused on her. She was wearing jeans and a white top, or something like that. It was too fashionable for that time and that area. A small bag hung on her back. On one hand she wore multicolored bangles, and in the other hand she held a notepad. She wore sandals and her fingernails as well as toenails were painted red. Her fingers were fair and thin, and I fell in love with her hands. Her black hair was parted and her face was the fairest I had ever seen. Her lips were pink and her nose was just perfect. Her dark black eyes shone bright. I was mesmerized. My Guddi had turned into a queen.

All my childhood I had dreamed of marring her, but that day I finally fell in love the moment I saw her. Guddi-mania overtook me. She was not human. I bet even the most beautiful fairy in heaven would be jealous of my Guddi's beauty.

She exited from the main entrance and stopped when she saw me. I looked at her. She looked at me and then in the other direction. Unlike today, girls were a bit shy in those days.

My urge increased, and I wanted to talk to her, but I was not in my senses. I was numb seeing the transformation in her. However, soon I was hauled back to reality.

I saw a boy come up to her. He held her hand and pulled her along. I took a step to reach out to her in order to rescue her, but I noticed she was smiling, so I stopped. The notepad and pen she was holding fell as the boy pulled her. She stopped and turned. I ran towards her to pick up her notepad and pen. She looked at me. I was lost in her beautiful eyes. I forwarded my hand towards her to return her belongings. I was on my knees. She forwarded her hand towards me to accept them and while exchanging her belongings, our hands touched. I felt a current running all over my body, the hair at the back of my neck stood. I felt the softness of her hands. I looked at my hands and heard a soft and melodious 'thank you'. By the time I lifted my head to say 'Don't mention it', she was gone.

I saw her at a distance. Holding the boy's hand, she was walking away from me.

A known personality once said, "When a man steals your wife or girlfriend, the best way to take revenge is to let him keep her." But lovers of our nation have no respect for the priceless advice of that noble man. And I am a lover from this very nation, so in jealousy, I decided to dishonor that noble man. I met Madhav and Harish and revealed my feelings to them.

"Just because I migrated somewhere doesn't mean that it's all over. I love her deeply and love never ends! And with separation, my feelings for her have become much more intense," I explained.

They hit me with jokes. They laughed. But I was serious, so I made it clear. "I'm adamant. I love Guddi."

Madhav and Harish looked at each other, surprised and shocked. They shook their head.

"But..." Harish took a step toward me and made an effort to speak and then looked at Madhav.

Madhav said, "A woman can be judged by her traits. As for Guddi, she is not the Guddi she was once in school when we all were together. She has changed a lot. She went through an overall transformation after you left. And it's not only her looks that have changed, but her soul too has passed through a period of transition, my friend."

"People don't speak well of her, man. Even we don't talk to her now. Childhood days are gone with childhood. Return to your Kanpur, and earn your living, or else you'll become like us villagers," Harish added.

I looked at the ground and listened to them in silence. I was half-lost.

"Just look at you. You're a working class man. And she is..." Harish frowned.

I continued to look at the ground beneath my feet. He was correct to an extent.

Maybe I am not deserving. But has love got anything to do with the word 'deserve'?

Harish continued, "By the way, you came here for Maa, I think." He sighed, "And not Guddi. Go. Run. Run away from here."

"Madhav, it is not for a man's judgment to peek into the trait of a woman, to know whether she is sterile or stained. I understand what you want to say, but love is everything it's believed to be. It really is worth crying for, fighting for, and risking everything for. I want to meet her once before I go. I want to talk to the one I wanted to marry once, and the one I love till now."

I smiled and continued, "I hope one meeting won't hurt much, Madhav. I've stopped here just to see her, whenever she comes here next. I'll leave after the weekend. And Harish, I also understand what you've been trying so hard to explain to me. But, my dear friend, when I had feelings for her during school days, I didn't understand it right then – the judging thing or the deserving thing. I was just a kid, and now it really doesn't matter. You know why?" I insisted.

Love is a damn powerful thing. If it happens, nothing else matters. It can turn even a dumb goat into a genius fox, and vice versa.

"Why?" said Harish. "You think that you're the only one sane here?"

"I love her for myself, not for people," I said.

As I waited for her arrival, I climbed the stone ramp that led to the top of the waterfall. From there, I could see the village at a distance. She'll be visible from here, no matter how far she is, I thought.

I had asked Harish and Madhav to tell Guddi that I had feelings for her. Madhav did as asked, and to my surprise and my wish, Guddi had agreed to meet me on her next visit home. Madhav also told me that she would meet me in the evening. However I left home in the afternoon. I was excited and mad with happiness. I decided to meet her at the waterfall because it was unlikely that anyone would visit the area.

From where I sat, I could see almost the entire area for a kilometre, including the road connecting my village with other villages, and the path from where I, Madhav, Harish, and Guddi used to go to school together till a few years ago.

The evening arrived while I was thinking what I'd tell her, and with evening time, a soft wind began to blow. Soon the wind got stronger, and I observed leaves fluttering. The wind had brought a delicate smell with it. It had bought the scent of a woman, which reminded me of my school days when I used to go to school with Guddi. It was her scent and it was nature's signal. She was only steps away from meeting her lover.

I saw someone diverting from the main road towards the falls. I stood, dusted my pants, and jumped from one rock to the other, to come down at the place from where a stream used to flow. I wet my hair and washed my face. I wiped my face and dried my hair with my mother's dupatta that I had carried with me as a lucky charm. Guddi was still on her way. I peered into the water to see my reflection and adjusted my hair to become presentable. Finally, after much waiting, my lady love had reached me.

She was wearing a blue jeans and a top, and had left her hair open. The weather turned instantly and black clouds shadowed us. Her hair blew in the strong wind. I stood there obediently, facing her. I had waited for hours, and planned for days, but now, I, the poor lover, didn't know how to start. Just then I noticed her sandals. One of its straps was torn. I took off my slippers, offering them to her. I faced her, standing barefoot, waiting for her to wear my slippers. But, she refused.

"What did you tell your friends?" she asked furiously, with anger bursting out from her lovely eyes.

Since when did Madhav and Harish become 'your' friends?

I realized how mistaken I was. Things were turning out to be different.

No 'Hi!' No 'How are you?' No 'Where have you been?' Nothing!
She started screaming as soon as she arrived.

I didn't answer. Instead, I asked, "How are you?"

How dare I not answer her, and instead ask a question? After all, she was a girl.

She didn't answer me.

"Please sit," I said, as I wore my slippers, cleaning a rock with my handkerchief for her to sit on. My voice was gentle, full of love and respect.

"I don't have much time." She was rude with an attitude, and looked away from me.

I persisted, and requested. She resisted, and only resisted. But then, after a while, she did sit down.

Girls, ego and...ufff!

I had sensed by the proceedings that circling and justifying was a waste of time and energy.

"Guddi, I know it's a bit weird, but dear, I love you," I said. I said it straightaway. I said it in one go, as I knew I'd never get the chance a second time.

She looked at me and then closed her eyes. And then she looked in another direction.

I continued. "When I was in Kanpur, I had seen in cinemas how some stupid actors cry after their beloved. During my free time, I had read in books how characters try to woo their love. And I had heard a lot of romantic songs on the radio. But it was all craziness to me until I fell for you. Once I tried to tell you during our schooldays, but couldn't gather the courage, and then I left the village after Maa passed away, so that I could forget everything and start afresh. It's not that I haven't tried, but the thing is, even though I tried, I couldn't do it, dear. I couldn't control my feelings for you, nor could I forget you. I love you. Please." I made a puppy face. "Don't take me wrong, Guddi."

I didn't know what I had done. I had gone there to meet her, but it was too late to realize that my feelings for her had overflowed.

She searched for words, and said, "Look, I am already in a relationship with someone. He loves me, and I love him too. His family has accepted me, and my family knows him well. It's final. I am his."

I am his!

Those words killed me. Right then. Right there. It struck deep inside my heart. My heart and lungs almost jumped out of my throat.

I sat there numb, looking at her.

I had no words to say or justify myself. All I did was that I showed her a portrait I had once made of her. Madhav and Harish had said, "Once she sees the portrait that you have made for her, she'll realize the depth of your feelings, and your good times will start." I too had the same viewpoint. But that day everyone was proved wrong.

As she saw the portrait, she sighed in anger.

"I need to go," she said. Her face was red.

I couldn't face her. I looked at the trees and bushes. The leaves were still – the wind had ceased to blow.

"Please stop," my heart said.

I wanted her to stay longer, but she was furious, so I kept quiet.

She turned and left. She walked off in her torn sandals, and I couldn't stop her.

It was all silent, except for the roaring water that was flowing. The waterfall yelled and cried for me. Its water was not ordinary water, but nature's tears, and its sound cries of nature for me!

There is no greater pain than unrequited love. For people who curse love because it has pain, they should know that pain is a manifestation of love. They really need to understand that if you can allow someone to destroy you, you should be able to allow them to create you as well. Love is not pain, but a path to pleasure; love is not betrayal, but a door open for certainty; and love is not nasty, but a journey that leads to everything nice. It is good to love, for therein lies its true strength; and whosoever loves much, performs much, can accomplish much. What is done in love is always well done.

The sun came down. And the birds returned to their nests. Darkness arrived along with the moon and the stars. And in different corners of my country most of the people would have reached home by then, after a whole day's toil. In short, things had changed, except the water falling from its height where I had waited for my love the entire afternoon.

Hours passed and I still sat there, buried in Guddi's thoughts. It wasn't that since I was heartbroken I wanted to jump into the water and die, but I just didn't feel like moving. It felt good to sit alone in the cold wind under the stars, surrounded by beautiful nature. Though nature was less beautiful than my lady love, I found peace there.

It was only after Madhav and Harish came searching for me that I realized it was almost midnight and Baba was concerned.

We three friends headed towards home. The path was wet. It had rained heavily that day after Guddi left. The clouds had also cried for me.

At home, as expected, Baba was very tense, but I had enough excuses. Giving him an excuse was nothing compared to the game I was in. I was playing the most dangerous game of all. The game of love.

J had watered all the plants, cleaned Sardarji's scooter, and had had my dinner. Sardarji was about to leave for home and sat on his scooter.

"*Are puttar*," he called out and I ran towards him.

I had arrived a few weeks ago, after extending my stay at Dhaneri to meet Guddi. However, her changed attitude had hit me hard. Madhav and Harish considered my leaving better, and since I had taken a month's advance from Sardarji, I came back.

"It came for you yesterday, I forgot to give it to you." Sardarji handed me a letter before he kick-started his scooter and left.

I gazed at the letter wondering who had sent it. I went to my room in the godown at the back of the shop and opened it under a lantern. It was from Guddi! What is left to say now, I thought as I opened it.

Dear friend,

I hope you are doing well. You must be wondering why I am writing a letter when I was so mean when we met last at Dhaneri. I am writing because later I felt I had behaved badly, and owe you an apology. I am writing this to apologize!

I understand your feelings for me, but I expect you to understand that love happens by chance; it doesn't follow a rule book or pattern. Nobody can force themselves into it, me neither.

You can write to me if you want, but write to the address I have written on the back of the envelope, because at home it's not safe. I'm in the hostel now, remember? The address written on the back is that of a trusted friend.

One more thing: as no one knows what may happen tomorrow, and it's not right to leave someone unsure, it's better we remain just friends.

Wishing you well for all times to come!

Your childhood pal,
Guddi.

Lord Krishna said in the Gita, "Do deeds without thinking of rewards."

I followed Krishna's advice and wrote back to Guddi. But neither Krishna knew, nor I, that in the real world, deeds are done for rewards only.

Dear Guddi,

I was doing well, but after reading the letter from you, I am now doing great and improving every single day. You must have heard of a famous writer Erich Segal. He wrote, "Love means never having to say you're sorry." And in our relation, I love you, so kindly drop the apology part, dear.

Well, I know I am being abrupt but this is how I am. Bye and take care.

Your childhood lover,
Mr Lover

I didn't think of Guddi's letter after that day. I became so busy in order to earn a living at Sardarji's that rarely would I think of the letter. But Guddi still lived in my heart. I was born for that love. I would think of her at times, not with hope, but of some good memories we had shared during childhood.

Today Sardarji abused me in front of all the customers. A crate of eggs slipped from my hands by mistake. The eggs broke and Sardarji went mad. It was evening time, so the rush was at its peak. He vented out all his frustration on me. I felt very bad. Don't workers like us have self-respect? Aren't we humans as well? Why does everyone behave with us so badly? It hurt me very much. But I understand. He must be facing some crises, for he is a good man otherwise.

I am fine now, though. Because something good happened. I can't sleep. If you can't fall asleep it means you are governed by a feeling called love. The triumph of dreams over reality.

Guddi had sent another letter.

Hey Buddy!

I can't believe it! Did you really forgive me?! You have such a big heart. You know, I thought you'd never talk to me, but now I feel so blessed.

I must admit I felt very bad and later, when we parted, I realized how right you were and how wrong I was. But I never tried listening to you. In fact, I misbehaved with you. And so, I really needed to talk to you.

And you know what, dear, after you left, things changed so much. I realized he was cheating on me – the guy I told you about. My family got to know about us and it was a mess at home. I was in big trouble and there was nobody by my side. I was deeply hurt, and so was my family. I wished there was someone understanding by my side, but I was all alone. I missed you so much man!

Hope I won't lose you now.

Your friend,
Guddi.

P.S. Couldn't sleep for many days after the day I got to know about his true colors. Trying to recover now. After all, at least you are with me now or so I hope.

I had thought she would never reply after reading such blunt words from me in the letter I had sent to her, but unexpected happiness surrounded me as I received another letter. This was just the beginning of a beautiful journey, because we continued writing to each other.

Hola!

How's life?

In your previous letter you wrote: "I'd have never done that to you, had I been the one." I know, dear. I know it very well. And that's why I wanted to talk to you.

I know you're a very good person. Everybody here in my college knows you now. I talk about you all the time to everyone. Life seems to be changing. As I had written earlier, I had forgotten to sleep, but now I sleep well. Your letters have become my lullaby.

My friends in class feel jealous of me as I have a person like you to write to. I wonder how things would have been without you; in fact, I don't even want to think of a time without you. I'm glad you're with me.

Write to me soon, else I'll stop sleeping again!

Your Heroine

P.S. I want you to be with me now, always, in any way you want. I don't want to lose your company again.

With that letter she had also sent her recent photograph. She was in a red suit, her head covered with a dupatta.

I read the letter twice.

Her letter clearly said that she had started enjoying my assistance, though we were far. But our hearts and minds were getting closer as the days passed. Falling in love again with my Madam was not a surprise. But Guddi was emitting rays of hope for our future as well. She had said in the letter that she wanted me with her, the way I wanted!

I pressed her photograph close to my heart, kissed it a number of times, and made a few sketches from that photograph the entire night. I kept a sketch each at every corner of my room and kept the original photograph under my pillow.

I wrote back the next day, and she wrote back very soon. In her next letter, she wrote about her future plans.

She was planning to shift to Delhi after her graduation. She wanted to live with her parents, but she knew once she completed her studies, they'd force her to marry. She needed some freedom for a while. She even wrote how restricting in-laws can be, and how much of a free life she wanted to live.

You will be free with me, my love!

I smiled as I read the letter, and kept it inside my wooden cupboard.

In the following letters that Guddi sent, she told me how much fun her college life was. Her list of college friends had reached eighty-nine. She liked romantic music. She didn't like reading books. She had seen a movie with her friends, though just about once. From poetry, painting, and designing, her interests had shifted to jokes, skydiving, and many others. In short, she had become extremely lively and active. Not to forget, very frank with me. I was loving it!

Guddi – my lady love would be a winner in every argument we would have, and more than that, I was happy to lose one every time.

A girl whom I wanted to see for hours, a girl who I wanted to listen to, a girl whose touch I wanted to feel, and a girl whom I had loved ever since I could remember had become the only reason for my existence. My love had deepened to the core and I wanted to spend my life with her ardently.

Dear,

Shall I confess something to you!? During the last years of school, I had also started developing a soft corner for you. But...time killed the happiness. And time has changed me so much that it's really difficult to trust someone again.

Anyway, I have news. One of my friend's friend is getting married in Kanpur soon. And she wants me to accompany her. Earlier I wasn't interested, but when she told me her story, I had to.

She is one of my classmates and a very good friend. She takes good care of me. Hope you understand. It's the wedding of none other than her guy. They love each other but are not getting married to each other. The guy's family won't accept her. And she wants to see him just once. I, along with a few friends, are joining her for support.

So, it's her story. And yes, I'll be there for two or three days. With great difficulty I've convinced Mom to send me, though Dad is not yet convinced. But I'm sure Mom

*will convince him by then, and they know if I wish to do
something, I do it anyway.*

Excited to see you soon!

Guddi

It had been many months now that we had been exchanging
letters. Guddi would write of many things – her friend Shashi's
birthday, the party and the presents she received. Guddi shared
everything with me. We would share experiences, photographs, and
emotions. There were times when we would write more than one
letter in a row, even before we received a reply to the earlier one.

Her next letter made me very happy, and gave me a new ray
of hope.

Oh Hello!

*What did you write – you're most welcome and you're there
for any help if needed? Obviously! You have to, mister!*

*I'll come a day before the wedding and as I don't know
the place, you have to help me shop. You have to show me
the city. After all, I'm coming all the way from Banda to
Kanpur for the first time. First time ever, alone, out of
home…can you imagine how it feels?*

*And yes, you too have to come to the wedding. Think
about the clothes we'll wear. You wear my choice, I wear
yours; we'll shop together.*

*For no reason, everyone here, ever since we've started
writing, says I've fallen in love with you. I think they've
turned crazy. But I do know that I love writing to you.*

Love,
Guddi

Girls are very good at it, but boys really don't know how to manage things. All my time revolved around her. Sometimes I would think of her, and sometimes prepare to write the next letter. In those busy times, I forgot Maa's words: "In order to win over your greatest dream, never forget about the smaller ones."

I forgot why I was there in Kanpur – for work. I had found something bigger than that – the reason for my happiness, for love, to live a life. And I was getting it all from Guddi. So, as a result, my mind was elsewhere when I was with Sardarji in the shop. I stopped showing up in the shop. All the time would pass in thinking and penning down my thoughts on paper. Whether it was day or night, I was always holding a pen and a paper. My wages had been reduced to half, and Sardarji had warned me a couple of times. In the past four months, I had not sent a single penny home. But who cares…for Guddi is with me.

Hey Guddi!

Is that so? I too am very excited to see you. In fact, more than you, if you ask. And don't worry, I've planned something for us – a big surprise. You'll love it!

By the way, I have nothing to do with what others say. I'd love to know what's your opinion about the 'falling' thing your friends talk about? Any plans about falling for me!?

Mr Lover

P.S. Please come soon! The wedding day is just a few days from today.

None can speak anything of time. Plans made in advance do not always materialise. Guddi's mother wasn't able to convince her father to allow Guddi to visit a different town without any elder from the house. This is what Guddi wrote in her next letter and all my hopes and plans came crashing to the ground.

I was virtuous, but not ascetic. I had faults, but was not evil. I was a common person who had become a crazy lover in search of happiness on the path of love. Love is a humorous topic for people who have not experienced it. To really know the best of love, one should ask the ones who have been in the game. They know how horrible a thing it can be. It might make you endangered and leave you defenseless. I didn't know before falling in love that when people are in love, they begin by deceiving themselves, and always end up deceiving others. I was in a state of ecstasy. And I was not ready to accept loss. I was ready to fight a battle.

Your father can stop you, but not me. Am ready to travel the world if it's for you!

I'm coming:

could-have-been-wife!	No.	~~could~~-have-been-wife!
would-have-been-wife!	No.	would-~~have~~-been-wife!
would-been-wife!	No.	would-~~been~~-wife
would-be-wife!	Maybe.	_?_-would be-wife!
my-would-be-wife!	Perfect!	

I'm coming *my-would-be-wife*!

Sanjay took a deep breath. He turned the pages to find if anything else was written at the back. Nothing. What happened after that that turned him mad, wondered Sanjay.

"All fine, son?" enquired Baba.

Sanjay nodded. He looked out of the window to check where they had reached.

"About to reach Dhaneri," Sanjay smiled at Baba. Baba smiled back. Sanjay collected the sheets and tied them gently with the ribbon. Maybe Madhav and Harish can tell me what followed, he thought.

Once he was back in Dhaneri, Sanjay ran to Madhav and Harish.

"We're not aware of such a thing, Bhaiji," said Madhav.

"Yes, I'm surprised why he didn't tell us," Harish joined in.

"But he never met you after he met Guddi, right?" asked Sanjay.

"He could have written to us at least," said Madhav. "How's he by the way? Any idea how much time it will take?"

"No." Sanjay sighed. "Even I want him to get fine soon. I'm so curious to know what happened next. He was so crazily happy to meet her."

"So are we Bhaiji," said Harish.

43

"He wanted to propose to her. From the letters it's clear that she had broken up with her boyfriend and liked Raju. Still, take the worst case scenario that she again rejected him." Sanjay looked at the letters.

"Yet becoming crazy doesn't justify it, Bhaiji. He lost his mother and he was rejected earlier as well." Harish looked at Madhav.

"Absolutely, he can't be so weak. There must be something else," Madhav said.

It was evening. They were sitting in a field. Sanjay looked at Madhav and Harish. "What do you do for a living?" he asked. "Any plans to work?"

Madhav and Harish looked at each other. Their silence was enough to reflect their unemployment.

Sanjay added, "Come to school from tomorrow onwards. Early morning! You are a primary teacher now."

"Primary teachers!" both of them said, looking amazed. They looked at each other in disgust.

Madhav and Harish reached the school early morning the next day. Though they were told they were primary teachers, Sanjay asked them to sweep the floor first. They did as commanded. And once the only teacher of the school arrived, Sanjay broke the news.

"They'll help you from now on. From teaching to cleaning to management...everything," said Sanjay to the old teacher and left.

Sanjay didn't stop after that. It was just the beginning. He stopped drinking, his attire changed and, unlike earlier, he started meeting elders and began participating in social gatherings.

It was just a month after he had returned from Dr Mishra's rehab that people had started praising him, especially after the day when he invited everyone to the village panchayat.

That day, for the very first time, Sanjay had attended the panchayat. The panchayat, as usual, was held outside school. Five judges sat under the tree, on a higher platform, and people sat facing them. The sarpanch wore a white dhoti and a kurta and had white turban on his head. He was in his seventies. Curling his thick moustache, he welcomed Sanjay and, on his behalf, the Sarpanch told everyone a few important decisions Sanjay had taken for the welfare of the village.

"I am honoured that Sanjayji is with us today. He has come for the first time, but with something that none of us had thought of had till now," the Sarpanch looked at Sanjay and smiled with a little bow. Sanjay joined his hands.

The Sarpanch continued, "Many of you don't know this, but Sanjayji is a man with a big heart. He called this meeting to let everyone know a few important things. It's a humble request from me that you all listen to every point clearly as they are for your benefit."

Everyone turned silent. They sat cross-legged on the ground and listened in rapt attention.

The Sarpanch began by reading some salient points from a piece of paper:

"One – As everyone knows, Sanjayji has farms of hundreds of acres outside the village, he proposes the people of our village to work on the farms there. Those farms have been lying barren since many years. They are open for farming now. People who are interested can meet Sanjayji anytime they wish.

"Two – Sanjayji has decided to help people financially at the time of need. If anyone needs financial help for a wedding, Sanjayji will help them with zero interest. And if both the bride and groom are above eighteen years of age, he will not take the money back. So, remember, eighteen years is what I say!"

The villagers looked at one another. Silence turned to chaos.

"Three – People who'll send their children to school and work on Sanjayji's fields will get double the wages, on a daily basis.

"Four – Sanjayji will support those financially who'll send their daughters to school..."

Sanjay raised his hand. The Sarpanch stopped midway and said, "Yes, Sanjayji? Do you have anything to add?" All the heads turned towards Sanjay.

"Ration to girls," said Sanjay.

People wondered what he had just said.

"Yes," said Sarpanch. "Also, people who'll send their daughters to school are eligible for more ration than mentioned in their ration cards."

"Marvelous," screamed one of the villagers from the flock. A few young boys whistled at the back.

The Sarpanch continued to read. "Five – Our school has classes till high school, but Sanjayji is making efforts to upgrade it to the intermediate. Also, a few young people like Madhav and Harish will teach in the school from now onward."

People screamed with enthusiasm this time.

"I invite other literate youth to come forward. Sanjayji has fixed a basic salary for them," the Sarpanch smiled. "Six and last – Sanjayji has proposed his help to students who want to study after intermediate and score well."

People clapped hard. One lady sitting beside Sanjay patted his back. Sanjay bowed thanking the lady. The Sarpanch talked to the other judges and concluded, "Today's panchayat is over. However, I would like to invite Sanjayji before we all take leave."

Sanjay went ahead. He turned to the audience and said, "Thank you everybody for coming here. To be frank, I had not expected so many of you to come, but now that you have, really, it's a big thing for me."

He smiled. "I was not in my senses for years, or so people say, and I think to an extent they were correct. But now that I am fine,

I think…" the listeners laughed in between, but he continued, "I want to bring about a certain change. I want to make this village a better village, a better society. Many of you would be thinking how I have become so enlightened." Sanjay looked at Madhav and Harish.

"There are three friends in this village who have done this – Raju, Madhav and Harish. Madhav and Harish are here with us, and Raju will be joining us soon. He's doing well. And yes – neither is he crazy nor has any bad soul entered him, so people please stop blabbering." Everyone laughed once again.

"Whatever Sarpanchji said a while ago is true. I have decided to take the initiative. I am thankful to the panchayat that for considering my ideas. Also, there are a few requests to make. If possible for you, say no to dowry, say no to child marriage, and say yes to education. Why not make one more Indira Gandhi or Rani of Jhansi from Dhaneri? Next week, MLA sahib is coming to Dhaneri…"

The crowd interrupted Sanjay's speech with hooting and whistles. He smiled. "Listen, he is not coming for fun. He's coming here for a purpose, so save that zeal for next week. He is coming to visit the school. I have talked to him and he has agreed to help Dhaneri with intermediate schooling and funds for a few basic necessities, but only if we have enough students to impress him. So, I request you all to send your children to school and be present next week, same time, same place, and yes, with the same zeal. Thank you all once again." Sanjay joined his hands into a namaste and bowed his head as the crowd screamed and whistled.

The following week the MLA arrived and people from within and around Dhaneri gathered in good numbers to welcome him. He was thrilled to see such a large audience and promised his support in every possible way. He asked people to have faith in Sanjay's words and support him in his cause. He added, "I had come here in greed of votes, but I am leaving with a pledge of change."

Sanjay's efforts showed results in a short span of time in the village. People approached him to work on the farms. The number of students in the school increased. The MLA kept his word and the school got the go-ahead for an Intermediate section. Children from other villages also joined the school. Few parents also came from a nearby village to ask Sanjay if he'd support their children who scored well in the Intermediate. Sanjay agreed happily. Not much, but a few sets of people, especially who were poor, sent their daughters to school, more for added ration than education, but also agreed to get their children married after eighteen, so that Sanjay could sponsor them. Not to worry about dowry was a bonus.

One day Sanjay went to school and asked Madhav and Harish to help him. "I have a few projects in mind. I'll need your help. Stay with me."

"Projects?" asked Harish.

It was recess. Sanjay, Madhav and Harish were sitting outside the school under a tree and the children were playing around.

"As I've decided to work for the betterment of this village," said Sanjay, "the MLA has suggested that I should enter politics."

"Politics!" Madhav said in amazement.

"Yes. And I have considered his suggestion," Sanjay smiled. "Everything that Raju has written in his journal, from the school to all the other practices that hamper the quality of life here...all that will be changed before he arrives."

Three Years Later

In the hot summers, the sound of crushing stones was making the ears numb. But even that was not able to stop Baba from thinking, thinking and thinking – thinking about the days of his life when he and his wife were expecting their first baby – the only son they ever had. They had dreamt to spend not even a single day without him. And then he thought about the day when his wife passed away. He had never thought her sacrifice would force her only child to where he stood – he was the one who became disturbed psychologically.

Raju was at The Home and Sanjay was the one who kept Baba updated of Raju's improvements. Baba was waiting for the day when Raju would come back. Days passed, but the feeling of happiness eluded them. Life would not have been worth living had Sanjay not been there.

But now things were all turning well. Raju was getting better, and finally they heard something good.

Dr Mishra had sent them a letter. As Baba had received the letter and read it, he ran to Sanjay to break the news to him of Raju's arrival.

"I'll go to receive him, Baba. You prepare to welcome him," Sanjay had said.

Baba agreed happily. In joy and excitement, he started arguing with Sanjay about the things in the house, about his attire, and about his own attire. He had turned energetic and childish out of happiness. Soon, both were quarrelling about trivial things and were laughing at them. Their happiness seemed to have turned the surroundings positive – the sun seemed to be shining bright, buds turned into smiling flowers, winds blew making a melodious sound and the entire village danced in happiness.

"What a lovely story," said Dia.

In his early twenties, wearing a red checkered shirt, white pyjamas, and slippers, Raju sat on a park bench. His eyes looked through black-framed spectacles, and his medium-length hair blew gently in the wind. Leaves fluttered and were falling to the ground while chirping birds maintained a peaceful chorus against a red sun slowly slipping beneath the horizon. The sky was beautiful, and the park too. Sitting on the ground were a few people who faced him, and were listening to him patiently. A few stood beside him as well. Everybody was lost in his words – words that formed his renaissance.

"Soon after, I was admitted at Dr Mishra's The Home and my treatment started. Sometimes doctors would give me shocks, sometimes antidepressants and sometimes new courses of injections would start. During the early days, I would sit alone in a corner, afraid of everyone. But as time passed, I showed improvement in my health. I stopped being frightened of you people here and became your friend," he said and smiled looking at everyone.

There were twenty-one people in The Home and each had his/ her own story. But everyone was there because of one reason only – love. Everyone was a patient of the heart, just like Raju. Everyone had dedicated their hearts to someone, but the person had rejected it. Kapoor Uncle's son had left him declaring him to be a drunkard and Kirron Aunty became crazy after being tortured by her husband.

Raju revealed that in real life, none of the psychiatric patients become mentally imbalanced by themselves. He found a few people at The Home who had more painful stories than his own. But it was from his own story that he had learnt a lot in those three years. All of his friends – Nana ji, Kapoor uncle, Kirron aunty, Sohail bhai, Zarine jiji, Ghuggi, John, Jacqueline, and the cute girl Dia – had also learnt a lot from him and his story.

Everyone hugged him. Some were even crying. Dia gave him a red rose plucked from The Home's garden. However, Raju didn't know how to respond to her. He was afraid of love by then.

"All fine now?" Harish tapped his shoulder.

"I was, but now that you've come, I'm worried a bit," giggled Raju.

"You won't change, will you?" Madhav joined in.

"For three years I did," said Raju, "and it seems you couldn't digest it."

Madhav and Harish laughed at Raju's joke. Standing at a distance, Sanjay looked at Raju. His wait of three years had come to an end. He walked towards Raju and his friends.

"Bhaiji…" said Harish. "This is Bhaiji."

"As if he needs an intro," said Raju and greeted Sanjay with a namaste. "I was your biggest fan a few years ago."

"I don't think I was Dilip Kumar," smiled Sanjay.

"But you were a great lover, I know," said Raju. Madhav and Harish looked at Sanjay.

Sanjay smiled. "People change."

"Where the hell is my son?" cried Granny, back at home.

Finally the day arrived of Raju's arrival but, neither him nor Sanjay arrived. The entire surroundings that had turned lively after years of mourning turned dull once again.

Granny continued, "You told me he was coming with Sanjay. Where are they?" She pulled Baba's vest and cried hugging him.

Raju's grandfather was sitting numb and Granny looked shattered. Only Baba had a bit of control over himself, but even he found it difficult to handle Granny.

"He will," said Baba. "I know it's been a long time, but my heart screams that he will come soon. And Sanjay will bring him. Because only Sanjay can make a miracle happen. I know he will."

"How can you do this, you selfish dog?" Harish abused Raju.

"Control Hari!" Madhav tried to calm Harish down.

"Then ask this selfish dog to think of the people back home. Why doesn't he get it that they've been waiting for light for so many years?" frowned Harish. "And so have we."

"Raju, what is this?" asked an irritated Madhav.

"Far better are these people in this rehab than the ones outside. At least they don't hurt someone if they don't love him or her." Raju's head was bowed down and his words were spoken softly.

"I'm afraid of stepping out. I feel safe here. I want to live with them here."

Sanjay didn't say anything. In his mind ran what Guddi's love had done to Raju. Madhav and Harish tried to persuade Raju to come home, but Raju didn't relent. He was persistent about his decision he had taken to live with his new family and make The Home his forever home.

In a very low tone, Raju said, "Love has the power to destroy all the forces by a mere touch. And when it is here in these rejected souls, why should I prefer that worthless world outside that is heartless?"

"Bhaiji, why don't you say something to this moron?" Madhav said to Sanjay.

"Ignorance of the law is no excuse and wanton sinful conduct is a crime, Raju," said Sanjay. "May I ask something if it's okay?"

Raju nodded.

"I read those pages that you had written once."

Raju looked at his friends in confusion.

"The doctor found it with you and he gave it to him," Madhav explained. "Yes, man! We almost forgot between the excitement and tension. What's with those sheets?"

Raju told them how he had developed the habit of writing after Maa's death. He revealed that till date he didn't know how she was taken away from him. When asked about the biggest mystery, about what followed after the journals end, he narrated his tale:

My heart pounded as I stood outside Guddi's college, three years ago. The wedding was an old story now. I had gone to propose to her on her birthday.

It was a great feeling, but I was nervous too. I spotted her near block number four, eating samosas with a few of her friends. She saw me, but cast her eyes away. I smiled and, with arms open like a hero, went towards her. By now I had become the center of attraction and other girls had become paranoid, but Guddi smiled. I smiled too. But you can never judge a girl's mood. She ignored me, and started leaving for her next class. I stood there for a minute, and then rushed to her. Pushing past around ten girls, I reached her. I put my hand on her shoulder and said, "Guddi!"

She stopped and turned. Before she could say anything, I wished her, "Guddi, happy birthday, dear."

I was nervous, very nervous, but I managed a smile. I went down on my knees and showed her the sketch I had made for her.

"Did you read it?" I smiled, pointing to the 'I Love You' with my fingertip. She looked at me gloomily for a while, and then moved forward. I followed her and held her hand. I became very desperate, and very persistent.

She shouted, "Leave me!" and freed her hand with a jerk.

She slapped me. She slapped me hard. I felt humiliated. With one hand on my cheek, I was lost and hurt, what had happened to her all of a sudden. Just then someone attacked me from behind. I was not committing a crime, but trying to woo my love, so I couldn't bear the indignity of the attack and stood up to retaliate. But soon, I was being dragged. By not one, but many guards, accompanied by a few boys. I didn't know what to do. All I did was swing my hands and legs in the air to free myself. Once out of the campus, a group of boys came running and thrashed me brutally.

I behaved like a real betrayed Bollywood hero that day for the first time. I threw away all the articles in my room in frustration once I got back home. My clothes, my mirror, utensils, some of the furniture Maa had brought with her as her dowry, all my documents of high school and intermediate school, including my mark sheets.

When I came to my senses, I felt pain in my back and noticed blood all over my upper body. The broken pieces of glass had drained much of my blood, and my back was still in intense pain as the pieces were still lodged in my body. Along with my shirt, the floor had turned red too. I stood up and threw myself into one corner where my bed was without even bothering to change, or even taking the pieces of glass out.

To love or be loved is to feel the torture from both sides. And unrequited love is not only torture for the ones who are in love, but to those as well who are with the ones in love. My family was shocked to see my condition. My love had become torturous for them as well. I didn't know how to explain my absurd behaviour. I seemed to have become blind. Clever are those people who learn from the mistakes of others, but I was a big fool. Not even by then had I realized the twenty-years-versus-twenty-seconds philosophy. I was crazy that I had fallen in love.

A few weeks passed. I had not put my foot outside home. All day I would lie in my room thinking of Guddi. She had been so friendly and loving in her letters, what had happened to her in college? She had not even enquired about me from Madhav or Harish. Doesn't a lover deserve this much of courtesy from the one he is ready to die for, I thought. This very thing was eating me from the inside. I was still waiting for her answer. I became deranged emotionally and mentally.

What else is life, but smiles and tears at the same time! It is such a great mystery. Just when we think we know it all, a wonderful new aspect shows up. The postman had brought a letter with him. It was from Guddi.

So she has taken the pain to ask about me and my health. Finally!

No sooner did I open the letter and read it, I fell on the floor. My spirit was crushed. I couldn't reconcile myself to what was written in it. I felt as if someone had thrown me down from the height of a thousand metres. I screamed, and sat on the floor, numb.

When I gathered myself, I cried miserably. I was lost. No thirst. No hunger. No senses. Later I hid silently in a cattle shed and after that day…

"But why?" Harish interrupted Raju's words.

Raju was still in the past as Harish shook him holding his arm. "But why? In the letters it was so clear that she had started liking you."

Raju didn't answer.

"Leave liking," Madhav joined in. "A slap is not justified!" Madhav was furious now.

"She was so excited to meet you, Raju. Isn't that what she said in the last letter that she had written to you? In fact, letters clearly reveal that she wanted your company, no matter what relation you both shared. She was in for anything."

Raju didn't answer. As sensitive as he was, he was shaken to the core. He buried his face in his palms. Sanjay, Madhav and Harish looked at each other. They pitied Raju, but couldn't understand the reason behind Guddi's behaviour.

"Now will you answer us, you jerk?" Harish expounded his irritation.

And once again, Raju didn't answer in words. However, he took out a piece of paper from his shirt's pocket and handed it to Harish. Sitting there with them, he, once again, buried his face in his palms.

It was a letter. It was a letter that caused Raju's destruction.

Harish read the letter and stood numb. His words followed a brief silence. "What the..."

Madhav read the letter and stood numb. His words followed a brief silence. "What the fu**..."

Sanjay read the letter and stood numb. His words followed a brief silence. "What the...*fuss!*"

Dear friend,

I know your mind is full of questions. Why did I behave so badly at the waterfall? Why did I write that apology letter? Why did I ignite fake hopes of love between us? Why didn't I pay any heed the day you were thrown out of my college?

Your mind has questions, questions and questions. But my letter has only a single answer. And it is this: "Hey rascal! I am Keshav, Guddi's boyfriend. She never wrote the letters. I did. Got it?"

How dare you think about my girl? How dare you even try to think of snatching her from me? Guddi is mine. You got it? She is Mine.

What did you think? By making a stupid sketch and writing worthless letters you'll win her over? You were wrong, man. By no means can you take her from me. So better forget her, or else the next time you'll receive a bigger shock. And trust me, it won't be words.

And you know what, Guddi never loved you. But from the day you created a scene in her college, she hates you like anything.

Guddi hates You! From the bottom of her heart.

You moron, so stay away from us!

Your childhood-lover's eternal love (Ha Ha Ha),
Keshav (Better remember the name, bloody loser!)

Though Sanjay understood a lot after reading the letter, he wanted to confirm if what he had interpreted was correct. He asked Raju, "What is this?"

Raju was sitting motionless. He finally replied, "The one I was in constant touch through letters was not Guddi, but the one she was in love with. Guddi shared my feelings with him, and he played with my feelings to take revenge on me for loving his girl."

Raju choked. "He has wronged me. And her. I felt connected to her, and so I felt pity. I felt the pain of a thousand bullets piercing through me and I was too shocked to face the truth. I couldn't take the pain she was causing me, and the pain I was subjected to. That's why I collapsed!"

Sanjay looked at Raju in a state of shock. "How could someone even think of doing it? It's so cruel!" he expressed.

"Bhaiji, it's not that I didn't have the wish to live. But to live, a purpose is needed, and that I didn't have. I was not just heartbroken, but heart-busted to read the truth." Raju sobbed. He sobbed for a long time and Sanjay let him. Not even Madhav and Harish tried to stop him. After a while, Sanjay hugged him. Madhav and Harish looked at each other in amazement.

Sanjay said, "I understand, but it's all in the past, my bro. Now wipe your tears and be brave."

Sanjay patted Raju's back. Madhav and Harish nodded. Sanjay, who was Raju's most devoted friend finally opened up. He tried to save him from the other depression he was fast entering into. But, under the pain in his heart full of agony, Raju still refused to listen to Sanjay. Then the drunkard conferred a gift to him by imparting to him wisdom, the path to devotion, and the doctrine of self-action. Whatever happened in the course of his life, Sanjay shared with Raju, to make him a better person.

Sanjay opened up, "Listen to what I say very carefully, Raju. I don't claim anything by telling you my story; I just want you to understand what life truly means. What it is to truly live."

Raju looked up at him with tears gleaming in his eyes. She wiped the tears off with the back of his hands and nodded.

So Sanjay began: "The only son of my rich parents, I never heard 'no' to any of my wishes. I got all that I wished for. Now all I needed was someone to love me and so my life was aimed at finding the one person I could love for eternity. Lucky me, I had found that person."

He smiled and continued, "She was my father's friend's daughter. We had met at one family function. And we fell in love! For her, love was everything. She would say, 'Fools disregard love, clad in human form, not knowing love as the greatest feeling in the entire human race. Those who don't believe in love don't have hearts. Those who don't have hearts can't breathe. Those who can't breathe are not alive. And those who aren't alive are called dead.'

"I used to feel so positive with her. They were such beautiful days, inexpressible! I spent an enormous amount of time and resources on her, and gave the relationship my best. I had been proud of my love and my relationship. But I never knew that only my love was eternal, not the relationship."

Raju, Madhav and Harish listened to him patiently.

Sanjay continued, "During a trip to her village, she revealed that her father had fixed her marriage to one of her cousins. Your first love is the perfect and only love, until you meet you second love, she had said, and married someone else. She said, 'The scriptures declare that if a lover dies for a righteous cause on the path of love, he at once ascends to heaven and lives for eternity. But, if you will not move ahead in this course of love, then, having abandoned your duty and fame, you shall incur sin. They, too, will recount your everlasting dishonor; and to one who has been honored, dishonor is worse than death. Having made pleasure and pain, gain and loss, victory and defeat the same, engage yourself outside for the sake of exploration; thus you shall not incur any sin.'

"That day I thought I won't commit a sin. I decided not to leave her either. I decided to set everything right, but I couldn't do it."

Sanjay's eyes were watering. He had shared his emotions with someone after many years. But in Raju's mind was a question. Taking his hand towards Sanjay, Raju asked in wonder, "Her father fixed her marriage with her brother?"

Sanjay wiped his eyes and said smiling, "Not brother, cousin. She was Muslim. We fell in love, and didn't know what to do. Though she gave me all the mantras, she was very tense herself, and utterly broken to hear her father's decision. So I talked to my parents, and guess what?"

"What?" asked all three at once.

"They agreed at once."

"Really?" Raju exclaimed with a smile. He had smiled for the first since they had started talking.

"Yes," continued Sanjay, "but her parents didn't. My father was a very good friend of her father's, as I said earlier. Papa told her father, 'You agree or not, I'm taking my daughter-in-law with me. Whenever you'll accept them, today or tomorrow, or years later, come to my village to give them your blessings.' Papa was not of this century, you know, and was very modern!" Sanjay was still smiling thinking of his father.

"Then?" enquired Madhav.

"The moment my father uttered those words, best friends of years became worst of enemies, and…" Sanjay stopped.

He didn't have the courage to speak further. He had ruined everything. But it was important to open up. It was important to let out all he had inside of him.

"And?" asked Harish. Raju looked at Sanjay. He was desperate to know what had turned an unconditional lover into a drunkard.

"And I lost my parents," Sanjay replied with a sigh. "They ended up in a fight. In anger, her family attacked the three of us with swords and threw us outside their village."

Raju frowned. Madhav and Harish were shocked beyond measure.

"Yes," Sanjay continued, "people know my story, but not the complete one. All these years I was not drinking in her memories…I couldn't gather myself ever after. I survived, but my parents died. I had no reason to live, but I lived just to show her and make her realize what her love had done, or rather her betrayal. Her love had forced me to incur a sin, that neither I nor she had wished for. That day I had decided to never return to the matters of the heart, but don't know why, when I heard of you, I did. I made it my aim to not let you be what I am. Because one broken heart is enough in one village. Right?" Sanjay managed a smile, wiping a tear.

Raju looked at Sanjay. Sanjay stood and started walking around, his hands crossed at the back.

Sitting there, the three childhood friends saw how sweet a companion Sanjay was to them. He had a soft corner for Raju. For him, Sanjay was an ocean of mercy and love. Raju saw a mentor in him. Raju stood and, joining Sanjay, he expressed his wish to show him the correct path in love. Madhav and Harish followed.

Sanjay told Raju that nobody can deny the fact that tears are a manifestation of love as well; no one can deny that in all the literature or reality of the world, there is no feeling so elevating and inspiring as love. It enables man to liberate himself from all limiting factors and reach a state of perfect balance, inner stability and mental peace, complete freedom from grief, fear and anxiety. But love, only love; not a crush, infatuation or even liking. Only love.

He said, "You're the one who has taken one stupid decision. You're a man of this century. And a man of this century has taken love to be not love, but something else."

"Something else! What?" asked Raju.

"A pool of desire," Sanjay answered. "You thought love is life, and so you waited for it, right? Right! You never realized just because you love someone doesn't mean they have to stick to you, all the time. Is love a condition? No! Love is not a condition to force your will. Is it a machine of smiles? No! They won't call it falling in love if you don't get hurt sometimes, but you just pick yourself up and move on. But did you? A big *no!*"

"But Sanjay, I have ruined everything in love. How can I rewrite it all? How can I make amendments?"

Sanjay explained to Raju that one who is regular in the act of love becomes free. He is the happy man in this world. He is not bound by anything. Not even karma.

"You don't need to regret the past. You were in love, and the one in love is free from all sins. He need not be reasonable or practical. He is accepted by the world the way he is. And no need for him to consider them or change himself for the ones who don't have the heart to understand his divine feeling."

Raju asked Sanjay whether he should go back into that inhumane, wicked and sadistic world. He persisted to let him be among the rejected ones and to stand by them and live for them.

He said, "For no one needs me outside, but they all need me here. My own love was never mine and now I don't even have a dream of loving again."

Sanjay rebuked Raju for his dejection, which was due to depression, and exhorted him to fight with that same world that is inhumane, wicked and sadistic. Sanjay took pity on him and proceeded to enlighten him. Sanjay asserted that only one who has the capacity to be balanced in pleasure and pain alike is fit for the divine feeling. He told Raju that if he refuses to fight and flee from The Home, people will be justified in condemning such action as unworthy of a lover.

"For the ones who have given me love and the ones to whom I have given pain...I don't have the strength to face any of them. How can I return to them? I committed a great sin that I had prepared to destroy my own family for my pleasure," Raju cried. "Alas!"

"Did you love her for pleasure? No! You loved her because you fell for her. Love destroys all not for pleasure of the body, but peace of the soul," explained Sanjay.

Having taught Raju the immortal nature of love, Sanjay turned to telling him about performing an action without expectation of fruit; lessons given in the Gita. He told Raju that a man should not concern himself about the fruit of the action, like gain and loss, or victory and defeat.

Madhav and Harish, looking at each other, followed Sanjay and Raju. They didn't utter a single word. In order to remove attachment which was the sole cause of his delusion, Sanjay taught Raju the imperishable nature of the love, the realization of which would grant him the freedom of the eternal. A doubt therefore arose in Raju's mind as to the necessity of engaging in action even after one has attained this state. To this Sanjay explained:

"Among enemies, it is hatred; among friends, it is joy; among children and parents, it's care and respect; and among lovers, it is love. It is the same thing. It changes according to time, situation, place and people connected. Above all, it is – a feeling!"

Raju listened to Sanjay, silently.

"Love is the soul of everything. Nothing can exist without it. And the soul that doubts on the path of love leads to destruction. Animals, plants, earth, me, you are all gifts of love. Aren't you? How can you say there's no love? How did you come into existence if there was no love between your parents? And the thing that is the greatest reason for your existence, you want to dishonor it? Why? Change your path. Prove yourself strong. Prove love strong. Fight with this world you call brutish, by moving out of here. And accept the fact: for certain is pain for joy and certain is joy for pain. Therefore, over the inevitable, you shouldn't grieve."

Sanjay stopped, turned, kept both of his hands on Raju's shoulders and, eyes fixed into his, he said, "Stand up and obtain all that is your birthright. Win the money and enjoy the luxurious life. Success, money, name, fame, and all the karmas – these are the things everyone should live for; for these are the birthrights of all humans. I couldn't live it, so I want you to do it. Step out and win your karma."

Raju turned around and sat on the ground. He looked into the sky at the innumerous stars shining brighter than ever. The soothing evening breeze chilled his ears. And he started playing with the stones. Sanjay looked at him, while picking up two stones lying nearby and, asked him, "What's this?"

"Two stones."

"No," Sanjay said, "this is your pain and sufferings, one each."

Raju looked at Sanjay in confusion. Madhav and Harish wondered if Sanjay was intentionally behaving absurdly to misguide the doctors so that he too could live with Raju at The Home.

Sanjay threw one stone. Now in one hand he held a stone and his other hand was free. Pointing out to the stone he still held, he said, "The pain and sufferings in life are like these pieces of stones whose absolute weight doesn't matter, but the duration you hold it for. If you hold it for a short time, the weight of the stone doesn't change; but the longer you hold it, the heavier it feels. You think about pain and suffering for a while, and nothing happens. You think about them a bit longer, they begin to hurt. And if you think about them all day long, you will feel paralyzed. It's important to remember to let go of your stress. As early as you can, throw all your burdens away. Don't carry them for long. Remember to throw the stones away!"

Sanjay showed them his free hand, and Raju thought how Sanjay's free hand was capable of doing anything, and how restricted his other hand was as it was holding that stone. Raju compared the episode with life and realized what one can make of one's life if one is free from all pain and sorrows. Raju realized it really was important to throw the stones away, or in simple words, to throw away all his pain and sufferings.

"Sometimes love comes into your life just to wake you up, not to stay forever. It comes to prepare you for all times to come. And, pal, the world thinks of me as a drunkard, and I agree that I am. But with it I am a person who has all this knowledge. For nine years I was not crying over my lost love, but learning these lessons. I have shared it with you so that you don't waste the remaining six and compete with me." Sanjay said with a smile, "Don't you dare compete with me!"

"But it's never easy to move on...do you think it's easy...can I?" asked Raju.

Sanjay's smile turned into laughter. He understood that he had convinced Raju.

"Who told you we are born to do only easy things? We are born to do difficult things, in easy ways," said Sanjay. "Look, love never gets in the way of fulfilling one's dreams. If it does, then it is not love. And if it's not love, it's not worth ruining yourself for it. Because love, and *only* love, is worth crying for, fighting for, and risking everything for."

Sanjay, Raju, Madhav and Harish arrived at Dhaneri the next day. Raju was astonished to see the change in Dhaneri. The biggest change was at the school. The school building looked better and the number of students had increased.

"Bhaiji has done it," said Madhav as they walked through school.

"Shall we go in?" asked an astonished Raju.

"Later," said Sanjay. "Your family has been waiting, bro. Let's go home first."

Raju nodded.

"Not only this, you'll find many changes in the village. Everything that you didn't like and had written about in your journal, Bhaiji has tried to fix," said Harish.

"Really, Bhaiji?" asked Raju.

Modest Sanjay didn't utter a word. He just walked along with Raju, Madhav and Harish.

"No more child marriages in our village. Can you believe it, Raju?" asked Harish.

"Really, Bhaiji?" asked Raju once again. Sanjay just smiled.

"For that, Bhaiji had to fight with even the Sarpanch. He met the MLA to convince the Sarpanch to stop child marriages in our village. In fact, in many other places, child marriage is banned now." Madhav joined. "And the biggest news is that Bhaiji has entered politics to bring a change in our society."

"It's good that my turning mad came in handy for Dhaneri in many ways. I was thinking I had wasted three years of my life," giggled Raju. Madhav and Harish joined him.

"These years have also taught you much, Raju," said Sanjay. "Best is the person who learns from his mistakes and works hard to make a better tomorrow."

Raju, Madhav and Harish nodded.

Madhav smiled and told Raju that they had also taken up a job at the school.

"What do you teach?" said Raju, astonished. "Bunking classes or smoking beedis?"

Raju and Madhav hi-fived. Sanjay felt happy to see the old friends happy. He felt at peace having set everything right for Raju and Dhaneri – a pledge he had taken three years ago.

The entire village had gathered to welcome Raju at his house. The place had been thoroughly whitewashed and the floor of all of the rooms had been washed twice. The house was decorated and men and women danced to the beat of drums and folksongs, while for the youth it was a day not less than the festival of Holi or Diwali. Colours, diyas, rangoli and a range of dishes added to the festive spirit.

Raju's grandma stood with tears at the entrance. She looped the aarti thali in circular motion in front of his face and smeared a pinch of vermilion, mixed with water, as a tilak on Raju's forehead followed by Sanjay, Madhav and Harish. She welcomed them in. Sanjay was no less than their own child now. He was the one who had convinced Raju to come home and had given Baba his life back.

Once all the friends, or brothers, were done with delicious dishes, Sanjay stood up to take leave. The family insisted he stay at least for a day, but he didn't.

"I've been with this idiot for a while," said Sanjay, "now it's your turn to tolerate him."

Raju accompanied Sanjay to drop him off. Madhav and Harish didn't join them this time. On their way to Sanjay's house, Sanjay asked Raju for the last letter. Raju gave it to him without being asked twice.

Sanjay took his hands at his back and smiled mischievously at him.

"What?" asked Raju, punching Sanjay on his stomach with a smile.

After a few seconds, Sanjay slowly brought his hands in front, and showed Raju the letter, torn into pieces.

Raju's smile disappeared.

"Why?" cried Raju. "It was the only memory I had with me of her – my love, my life, and my reason for existence."

"And it was the only thing..." said Sanjay, throwing pieces of the letter into the air, "that dragged you to hell. Had there not been this letter, you would have never gone to The Home."

Raju stood there, numb, listening to Sanjay.

Shaking his head, Sanjay continued, "Almost all betrayed lovers keep material things of their lovers as memories. Morons! Why? Why don't you understand one simple thing that memories stay in the mind, or sometimes in the heart, not in some materialistic thing. All it needs is strength of a few seconds to destroy all material things you have with you, and once you have done it, trust me, life will start turning better. And trust me, pal, from now on, after I have torn the only memory of her in form of that letter, you'll discover a new thing every day and life will end up the way you have always dreamt. You have my word!"

Raju didn't say anything anymore and smiled. He hugged Sanjay.

Raju said before they parted, "A very big thank you for saving me. I think I should leave now. I have to make amends."

One Year Later

Sitting at the reception of Kaizen Internationals, he looked at the walls. There were boards with pictures, messages, goals, steps to success, organizational heads, pictures of the CEO and his small bio-sketch. As Raju waited for Sridevi to get free, he started reading the annual magazines of the company.

Office timings were from nine in the morning to five in the evening. Raju woke up early that day and reached the office before time. He wore the best clothes he had – a white shirt with blue vertical stripes, navy blue trousers, and black shoes.

He reached the office fifteen minutes early. He saw a juice corner outside the office and decided to have a glassful of juice. By nine, he was at the reception area of the office.

There were three receptionists at the reception, out of which two were very beautiful. He went to the least beautiful of the three.

"I'm here to meet Srideviji, Business Head of this company. She asked me to meet her," said Raju.

Sridevi and her team were busy with interviews so he was asked to wait. He sat on a chair in the reception.

Sanjay's words had given Raju enough strength and motivation, and had encouraged Raju to come out of his grief and transform himself. Once convinced that he would face the world, Raju expressed his feelings to move out of the village. Of course,

Baba refused. But thinking about his future and listening to Sanjay's words, they agreed.

"It is very important for one to get exposure. Though there is a risk and danger away from home, but then, it's just about everywhere. How safe was he when he stayed here? For sure one has to go through a lot when he is away, but those experiences only teach him about life. Life does take you to a better place, if you only try. And a soldier is safest when he's not at the front, but then, that's not what he's meant for!" Sanjay had said.

His family's love and Sanjay's support had put a lot of sense into him and made him a new person, a transformed one. Raju was more confident and focused now.

He never turned back towards sadness, or pain. Guddi was always in his heart. Her memories remained. And it was only she who kept him still, and kept him determined.

A new person with a new mentality now, the first change in a new Raju was work – work hard, grow more and make your own identity. Earlier, all he wished for was food, cloth and shelter, but now he needed to do a lot, and own a lot. Now he wished for a lot more.

It had almost been a year since he began working in Bombay. The early days in the city were tough. He spent some of them on the roadside, but soon, with the help of a contractor, he got a job of a salesman. He had to go home-to-home in order to sell gas lighters and gas pipes. He would go to different houses and sell his products. In the afternoons, when people would be resting in their houses, he would hit motels where people would go for lunch. So he would sit outside motels and stop every person going in and coming out to give him a minute. Not everyone entertained him, but then there were a few kind ones who purchased the products from him. There were some cruel ones too, who insulted him. But he never gave up. He gave his best. He had discovered few methods to increase his sales. And lessons from Sardarji in Kanpur helped him deal with all kinds of customers. Putting them together, things began to work for him and he started earning good money.

A few days earlier he had done some calculations and concluded that if he continued to work every day as he had been working since a year, it would take him a lifetime to become a rich man. So he started striving for something better. He went for an interview at Kaizen Internationals and was selected.

This was his first day, his meeting with Business Head Sridevi Shastri. As Raju waited for Sridevi to get free, he started reading annual magazines of the company. After some time, the phone bell on the reception desk rang, and one of the two beautiful receptionists asked Raju to accompany her to Sridevi's office.

He had never dreamt that he would work in such a big organization. He was literally trembling.

The receptionist knocked on the door.

"Come in," a voice came from the inside.

The receptionist opened the door and Raju entered.

"Come. Please be seated," greeted Sridevi. "Our HR team and Manager have praised you a lot."

Raju thanked her with a smile and took a seat in front of her. He looked at the office. It was a big room with Sridevi's desk in the front, a luxurious sofa set on one side, and a bookshelf on the other. The room smelled pleasant and though it was summer, and though in those days an air conditioner was not an easy appliance to afford, her office was cold.

A few trophies were displayed behind Sridevi's chair, and on the walls were a few portraits of legends in the business world. The room itself was a source of inspiration.

"I was busy, so sorry that you had to wait. I hope you were taken care of?" she continued the conversation.

"No. I'm okay." He was very nervous.

"Means my staff didn't take care of you?" she frowned a bit.

She phoned the reception and the receptionist arrived in a few moments.

"He will work with us from today," said Sridevi to the receptionist and turned her face to him, "or tomorrow onwards." She then again turned to the receptionist and said, "I hope he was taken care of with respect."

The receptionist looked at Raju apologetically, her head down. Sridevi's eyes turned ashen.

"Ma'am..."

The beautiful receptionist was about to say something when Raju interrupted, "Coffee was wonderful Miss...?"

Receptionist stood quiet, her eyes still down.

"Miss...?" Raju stressed requesting her name.

"Usha," she replied.

"Miss Usha, I'd like to have the same coffee every morning." he smiled.

"Sure," she thanked him for saving her with her smile.

"That was nice, Usha. Thank you," ordered Sridevi.

"Sure ma'am," she said and left.

"You saved one employee today," Sridevi said when the receptionist left.

Raju turned to Sridevi, as he was still looking towards the door that Usha had just shut. He gave her a smile.

Sridevi phoned the reception. "Ask someone to bring in two cold coffees."

"So sir, are you ready to join Kaizen Internationals?" she came back to him.

"Yes." He sat with his head held high with confidence.

"Good. So let me give you a brief intro of our company and its mother company, followed by what you are supposed to do," she said, and told him all the necessary details.

Kaizen Internationals was a sub group of GrowingWings Group. The Mother Company, GrowingWings Group was started by two brothers in 1969 in Australia. They had no resources to manufacture their own products, and a new product takes time to spread in the market and create a niche for itself. They found that marketing of already existing products is safe for an early stage of entrepreneurship. So instead of manufacturing their own products, they tied up with a few companies to sell theirs, demanding some fixed percent as return per sale. They tried and it worked. After a few years, in 1972, one of the two brothers went to the United Kingdom and started the same business. It worked wonders in the UK. They handed over their business to a panel of selected business heads in UK, and themselves went to different countries to spread their business. India was one. It took them some years to reach India, but once they did, they tied up with many private sector companies.

The company was active in twenty-six countries when Raju joined. There were twelve business heads in the different cities of India. Sridevi was Business Head of Mumbai, or Bombay, as it was then, working with more than a hundred people under her.

The cold coffees arrived.

Raju picked up one glass and they continued while sipping their coffees.

"Hope you'll like the work here and will be satisfied," said Sridevi.

"I think I'll never be satisfied," said Raju. "The day I'll be satisfied, my thirst for more will die. And I don't want it to die. I want it to grow more and more in order to achieve more and more."

"Interesting!" she exclaimed. "Manager Anil will soon be here. He'll see to your queries if any. Enjoy your coffee till then."

Eventually there was a knock on the door and Manager Anil entered.

"Good morning, ma'am. It seems like a really good day. Hope winds for Kaizen will blow from different directions," he said looking at Raju.

"I have told him about the organization and the mother company. I have also told him about his work and the expectations we have from him. Kindly make sure he doesn't miss out anything," Sridevi instructed Anil.

"Sure ma'am," he nodded.

"What do you think of failure?" Sridevi asked Raju.

"An opportunity for the future," Raju quipped with a pause, "When one door of happiness closes, another opens; but most people often look at the closed door. They don't see the door that has been opened for them. One should be alert, always. Opportunities knock not once, but many times, ma'am."

The lady looked at the manager, astonished.

She said, "Good. When he was asked this question, he said he'd feel depressed when he loses." She pointed towards the man sitting beside him.

"Depends on person to person, ma'am, and his thinking too," said Raju, turning his head towards the man. "Well, no one can make you feel inferior without your consent."

"Yes," she agreed. She banged the table with her fist. "And what do you think about customers? Customers are gods to business people."

"For me a customer is a fool," replied Raju.

"What?" said both the lady and the man in unison.

Raju took them by surprise.

"Yes, fools. Business is all about fooling people. Especially marketing. Every business is good and every product is not the best, and so it works. Why? On one simple principle – fooling a customer. When you are new, you don't know how to sell anything, but experience teaches you to do so. It doesn't teach you about the company or about the product. All it teaches you is how to fool people."

They laughed at his reply. Turning to Raju, the manager said, "Shall we?"

"Thank you, ma'am," Raju forwarded his hand to her.

"So anything you want to know?" the manager asked as they headed towards the door.

"If I want this...or such an office, then what do I need to do?" Raju asked.

The manager laughed and turned back to Sridevi. "Ma'am, his first query is what does he need to do to own an office like this."

Sridevi laughed as well. Raju was embarrassed. It was not a joke, but he guessed the question asked by a to-be-salesman was inappropriate.

Sridevi stood from her chair and said, "Come Mr Ambitious, I'd like to answer that question."

She went to the wall in front of her table and she showed them a large chart hanging on the wall. She started explaining as Raju listened, terribly alert.

Chairman

CEO

Country Head

Business Head

Monthly target: 100000 units
Group near 100

Senior Manager

Monthly target: 60000 units
Group:45 to 50 people

Manager

Monthly target: 25000 units
Group:10 to 12 people

Sales Officer

Monthly target: 6000 units
Group: 5 to 6 people

Sales In charge

Monthly target: 1200 units
Group: zero

Salesperson

"You are a salesperson, or will be once you get a job letter. You'll not be permanent. Salespersons are non-permanent in our company and get a rupee and fifty paise of every ten rupees they sell. You can take it as a training period and consider yourself to be a trainee. There is a Sales In-charge above you who manages a group of five to six people, and he is under the Sales Officer, who is under a Manager and so on. Sales In-charge will teach you your work on the field and is responsible for you. Obviously we all are, but not always. He is the one to question when you have any problem or sales are going down. Your target for a month is 1200 sales. Once you hit the criteria of 1200 sales for a month, you'll be promoted to Sales In-charge. And for that month, your leader i.e., Sales In-charge gets a commission for the sales you did for that month. As there is a big role of your leader in your success, our company gives them this gift when their juniors are promoted. Your senior gets a reward for the work they did on you, and you become permanent in our company. Now once you have been promoted to Sales In-charge, you have to manage a group of five to six people, as your senior was doing earlier. Your Sales Office will be the person you'll be dealing with now. Then, once your group collectively hits the criteria of 6000 sales in one month, you will be promoted as Sales Officer, with a group of ten to twelve people to handle. And like this, a person grows in our company. Even I joined the mother company as a salesperson, years ago," explained Sridevi.

It was Raju's first day, but he was feeling very involved in the workings of the company.

"How much time did you take to become a Business Head?" he asked Sridevi, his eyes still focused on the chart.

"Stop dreaming about Business Head, sir. Your first target is getting permanent and being promoted to Sales In-charge. Sales alone are very difficult to manage. Most people leave this job when thcy don't find it possible, and for this reason we have decided to keep salespersons non-permanent…so that they give their best, and once they start loving the work, they become permanent. But for your information, let me tell you, we have the most dynamic Business Head in India. Ma'am took three months to get promoted to Sales In-charge, while I took nine months," manager Anil interrupted them.

"I think, it took ma'am about seven years to reach at that level. Ma'am has reached the position the fastest in India after two others from abroad. Ma'am's next target is Country Head. There is only one Country Head in one country and thousands of people work under him. In India we don't have any Country Head right now, so a panel of Business Heads is looking after the business. Right ma'am?" Manager Anil seemed to be buttering Sridevi.

"Absolutely right, Anil. But there is time for that glory. Don't know how many years!" Sridevi sighed.

"That's great. But the criteria of becoming the Country Head is not mentioned. How will you become Country Head, ma'am?" Raju dared to ask.

Sridevi looked puzzled.

"I don't know," she said. "And Anil forgot, but not only India, none of the twenty-six countries where the mother company is working has a single Country Head. Once, the Chairman and CEO of the mother company said at the conference held in the US: 'When we see that someone deserves it and is working more than expected, we will draw the criteria.' No one has been able to win the Chairman or CEO's trust, so everyone has to wait."

Anil rubbed his head, outdone with the proceedings.

"Who are the Chairman and CEO?" Raju asked.

"The two brothers who formed the GrowingWings Group," replied Sridevi. "The elder one is Chairman and the younger one is CEO."

Finally, with that, the day ended for Raju at the office.

Anil and Raju came out. The receptionists were still surrounded by paperwork, and he along with Anil went out for lunch to a nearby motel called Lucky Dhaba.

He got to eat some delicious food while somebody else paid the bill. It was a fitting end to his first day at work.

He wrote two different letters with the same matter recounting his first day at work, one to his parents and the other to Sanjay.

Baba and Sanjay were still living in Dhaneri. It had been more than a year since Raju had met them. They had been constantly asking Raju when he'd be coming, but he had no plans to go to Dhaneri. They were okay with their lives, and he was happy with his.

Every morning, all the employees of Kaizen Internationals would assemble in the common room to attend a meeting, applaud the high rollers (the ones who made highest units of sales the previous day), and discuss the plan for the day. The meeting would go on for around an hour. After the meeting was over, everybody would leave and head towards a dhaba. It was breakfast time. And when Raju would be rather bored and partly exhausted around eleven, everyone would leave to begin work.

If you can stay calm while there is chaos all around you, then you haven't completely understood the seriousness of the situation. Raju hated morning meetings. For him, those two precious hours from nine to eleven were a waste. According to him, the company should have changed the office hours from eleven to five, and morning meetings should have been held only once a week or twice a month. But it went on like that and he had to be a part of it.

Luckily, he got a very talented Sales In-charge in Maya. She had been working in the company for the last eight months and was newly promoted. She used to be a high roller. She was helpful and worked after five on the field. The only thing Raju didn't like about her was the time she would waste on one client. Rather than sticking to business, she would talk of everything else and have lengthy chats with them.

One day a woman was telling Maya, "I made my husband a millionaire."

Raju asked, "What was he before?"

"Billionaire!" the woman replied.

Holy hell!

The new job was quite different from the previous one. Rather, the customers he dealt with were different, and this Raju realized after he made his first deal.

It was 3 May. He remembered his first customer for a long time. His name was Viney Dhall, and he was from Haryana. He belonged to Salara Mohalla in Rohtak and had been working in Bombay for ten years. It took Raju some time to take Mr Dhall into confidence, but he did win eventually. The real war was with his second customer, Mr Munish Datta. It was two days later, on 5 May. He spent an entire afternoon in Mr Datta's office. It took Raju hours to convince him that Kaizen and he could be trusted, and that he'd earn huge profits. Mr Datta told Raju how he had been betrayed by many professionals earlier, but Raju did take Mr Datta into confidence, and they signed the deal. Mr Datta was an engineer working in Bombay for some thirty years, and was originally from Mohali in Punjab. Very few people were that literate in those years. Not everybody was an engineer like present times.

One month passed, and Raju was not doing well. He put in a lot of effort that entire month, but his sales reached only 200 units. The money earned was enough, but he was still temporary. To become permanent, he needed to put in six times more effort. But he was already giving his best.

Every day, from nine in the morning to nine at night, Raju was on the field, trying his luck and nurturing his abilities. Every night before going to bed, he planned a new strategy, and the next day, he'd start implementing it. Sometimes he worked without a break and sometimes he worked with breaks, recharging himself. Sometimes he tried to make a deal with every person he met and sometimes he judged the person first. With new ideas, he jumped to break his previous record, but in vain.

Love is such a powerful drug; it is hard to run away from. During some moments, Guddi's thoughts crossed his mind. But controlling his feelings, he kept them aside and focused on his sales.

His sales for the second month were 180 units, even lesser than the first. In the third it went to 250, in the fourth it was 245, and fifth it was 237. He tried hard, but nothing seemed to be working.

Sridevi had hit her first target in three months, Anil had hit his first target in nine months, and Maya in six months. It had been ten months and Raju had not even reached half of the number of required sales. He thought: if I will move like this, it will take years for me to become permanent.

Maya was working hard and her stars seemed to be working, Anil had been promoted to Senior Manager now.

Baba along with Sanjay continuously forced him to meet them once. Raju stopped sleeping in his stress for meeting his target, and as a result, fell sick. So he took leave for a week.

For seven days, he did nothing. He just ate and slept. When you don't have much to do, and things are not in your favour, the best step to be taken is to sleep. Give your mind some rest, and then miracles will follow.

"Usha, I hope you know it's not a date," he said.

On Sridevi's birthday, she gave a party to all her employees. At the party, Raju met Usha, the receptionist he had saved on the first day at the office. They had met after a long time. He had never been in contact with her. Not even for that coffee that he had asked for in Sridevi's office.

Raju had never gone out with anyone, because all the time, Guddi's thoughts ruled him. That day, he asked Usha out. They met at the same motel – the lucky one for him.

"What can I do for you?" she asked.

She seemed interested, so he felt more comfortable and the way seemed easier. He opened up easily.

"You know Maya's rival Neelam?"

They were sitting opposite each other.

"Obviously," she said, and kept both of her hands on table to come closer.

"And Govind? One of the members in Neelam's group. He is new and is not making much from sales," said Raju.

"Yes. He is planning to leave, I think. He is finding it tough. Sales for him are not working," replied Usha.

"I want to help him," he said, "with your help."

It was evening and the ambience of the motel was breathtaking. And there was something special in the air. Don't know what, but there was something – something that was missing the first time he had come.

"What do you want to do?" Usha demanded.

"Ask him not to leave the job. I'll give him my sales in his name for this month. He'll get good money from the company for that. Kindly ask him to sign the papers."

"And what about you?"

"I have secured some money. It will do well for this month."

Raju was happy to help Govind, though he was from the opposite team and a rival.

"You are so good dear. I'll do what you said," said Usha.

He felt the 'dear' seemed a bit romantic, but that was not the concern right then. He was there for a task, and that was done.

Usha agreed to do the favour for Govind, and Raju felt relieved. He had done something that gave him satisfaction. His heart felt happy and wise to help someone. Usha was such a wonderful girl. She possessed beauty in her heart as well. She was ready to help Raju in a cause.

The next day, Usha went to Govind and gave Raju's sales documents to him. Govind saved his job. And Raju saved his dream.

One month later, Raju asked Maya out for dinner. Same motel. Same time.

According to everyone at the office, she was hitting the target of a Sales Officer that month, but that day she revealed to Raju that she was a few sales short.

"How much?" he asked.

"Thirty," she replied, sad.

"Don't worry. You are a hardworking person. You'll make it next time," he sympathised.

"When?" cried Maya. "When? Who knows when my team will reach close to six thousand again? For the last six months, I was doing four thousand. It was after seven months that I reached five thousand. I had already lost a chance a few months back. And then I don't know whether the next chance will come after a month, year, or life," she said frustrated.

"Don't worry. I'll do something," Raju comforted her.

"What will you do?"

"Trust me once. Just this time, and you'll see a miracle on the final day," he said.

They had dinner and parted. Raju was sad because of his sales. Maya was sad because of her sales. But their rivals were happy. But Raju's last cause, Govind had improved. He worked well under constant supervision and cornered a rat in a trap. Neelam and Govind were happy, while Raju had more plans.

I love her smile, her face and her eyes; damn, I'm so good at telling lies! Romance with a working colleague is not a good idea!

The day after he met Maya, Raju asked Usha out for dinner again. This time she brought along a shirt for him. He was so surprised. He refused to accept it, but she insisted.

"If you really want to present me with something, then help me," he said over dinner, trying to refuse the gift she had brought.

"How?" she enquired. "I will. Plus, you can keep it anyway," she persisted.

Usha had developed a soft corner for Raju after he had saved her from Sridevi. His colleagues teased him with her, but he was too busy and involved in his work to give it any thought. However, that day he did sense it. The way Usha had dressed, the way she blushed, the gestures, and the gift she had brought made it apparent that she had feelings for him.

"How are Neelam and Govind?" enquired Raju.

"They are great. Govind is out of this world these days. He thinks I like him and so I arranged sales for him the previous month. I told him that he is a good friend and didn't want him to leave the job, and that's why I helped him but he has made up his mind. He frequently tries to woo me." She blushed. "I hope you are okay with it?"

Raju was not her boyfriend, so he wondered why she had asked him that question.

"Not at all. After all, it's your life. The one concerned should be you, not me," he said in a straightforward manner and asked, "Anyway, tell me how many sales I gave him last month?"

"Two hundred I think. I don't remember exactly."

"Can you ask him to give thirty sales to someone? He will not lose anything. On the company's documents, he will update thirty sales in someone else's name, but I'll pay him the cash for those sales."

"Obviously he will. What problems will he have? In fact, anybody will do it," she said with confidence.

"Okay then, kindly ask him to do it, and I'll give you the money."

"I'll tell him to update it in your name, but why don't you give the cash yourself?" she wondered.

"I don't want to come into the picture, that's all. And yes, update it in Maya's name. Not mine."

"I will," she said.

She blushed again and started looking into his eyes. He didn't know how to respond. All he did was smile, because that was spontaneous.

The Business Head and other managers were on stage. It was the day when promotions for the month were to be declared. They all were in the company's auditorium and the names of those employees were to be announced who were to be promoted.

Two people were getting promoted. No one knew the names. But Raju knew one name – Maya. He was happy for her, until she gave him a shock when she arrived.

"I don't need thirty sales. I need fifty. One of my clients returned the order, so my figures have gone down," Maya broke the news.

It was too late. They all were in the auditorium by then. Sridevi and all the other seniors stood right in front of them. Even the sales from Govind had not come through as he had not heard from Usha after the dinner.

I hope she has not run off with my money!

He was tense as all of his efforts were being swept away, because even if Govind gave his thirty sales to Maya, she wouldn't make it.

"You all know there are two promotions this month. But any guesses what the names are?" Sridevi screamed out of enthusiasm.

The crowd in the auditorium shouted out different names, out of which Maya was one. People looked at Maya. She knew it was not her. She looked at the people and smiled.

"Mithun Khan," screamed Sridevi. "Mr Khan has been promoted to Sales In-charge. It took him a complete year to get promoted and his sales figures are 1234."

Mithun went up to the stage and stood beside Sridevi. Everyone applauded. He was from other group and had joined with Raju. Raju felt disappointed with himself.

You are left behind, Dumbo!

"Guesses for the second promotion?" Sridevi screamed once more. People looked at Maya. She knew it was not her. She looked at Raju. Next time ma'am, he thought.

"Maya Kaushal!" screamed Sridevi.

Maya couldn't believe it. Nor could Raju. She looked at him, and this time he smiled.

Sridevi continued, "Miss Kaushal has been working for a while with us and has been promoted to Sales Officer from Sales In-charge. And you'll be surprised to know that her sales are exactly 6000. A single sale less and, she would not have made it this time."

People applauded with much more enthusiasm this time. They were still looking at Maya. A miracle had happened. Her eyes were shut and her head faced the ground. Her eyes were moist.

Raju went up to her. With one hand he patted her back, and with the other he held her hand. She held his wrist. She knew he was responsible for the miracle.

"Your time has come, Mayaji. Go on and snatch what you deserve. Go," Raju commanded, while he wiped her tears.

Maya ran up on stage, smiling, and once he saw her smiling on stage, with Sridevi and the other bosses, tears rolled down his own eyes. A few years ago, he was destroying his life for someone, and today he had brought a smile to another person's face. He felt proud of himself. His heart felt happy once more. He wiped his tears with one hand, and found the other clasped by someone. To his surprise, Usha was holding his hand.

*U*sha holding his hand was a shock for Raju. But then there were good things happening after such a long time, so he didn't give it too much thought.

Govind had felt emotional when Usha updated him of Maya's need. Usha had told him that, being in a different group and being a rival, Maya had given him her sales the previous month when people of his own group didn't even think of it. And instead of thirty, Govind submitted fifty sales to the company in Maya's name, and that changed the entire course for Maya's promotion.

Govind even returned the money Raju sent. Raju threw a party for Maya's success with that money. The party was held at Raju's lucky motel and he invited only the people of his group along with Sr Manager Anil, Business Head Sridevi and of course, the cutest girl in the office, Usha.

Raju was not Maya's junior any longer, he had become her best friend. After all, Maya was promoted to Sales Officer because of him.

"In a professional set-up, even your blood relatives can become your enemies, but without thinking of yourself, you did so much for me. You won me over today," she had said that evening at the party.

And yes, how could he forget that at Maya's promotion party, Usha stared at him continually during the entire evening. While she was leaving, she said, "The person you'll get married to will be the happiest, dear."

When he started a journey, he had known just one girl whom he loved, dreamt of, and tried hard to chase; but today, time had changed to an extent that two different girls were chasing him at the same time. He was being showered with blessings. In short, Raju had won two ladies in a day.

Yippee!

They resumed their work for the current month.

His friendship with Usha and Maya didn't affect his performance. The only difference he found was that he had started calling them by their names, without using 'miss' as a prefix or 'ji' as a suffix.

"The day I was promoted, I had nothing in my bank account, and you threw a party for me. I wanted to make my parents proud, but couldn't. You did it for me. I was promoted because of you. Thanks dear," said Maya.

He was with Maya at the Lucky Dhaba.

The following month after Maya was promoted, she asked Raju out for dinner when she got her salary.

She was very emotional that day.

"A friend in need is a friend...so and so," he said and smiled. "By the way, do you know what happened on Sr. Manager Anil's birthday? I've heard something."

He tried to brighten up her mood by changing the topic.

"No," replied Maya.

Raju told her in detail. "On his fortieth birthday, he went down for breakfast knowing his wife would be pleasant, would wish him and would give him a present, but she didn't even wish him a good morning, forget happy birthday! He realized that distance increases in relationships with age. He thought at least his children must have planned a surprise for him, and waited for them. Soon the children came down. He looked at them with a smile, expecting something, but the kids had their breakfast, and left for school."

"So what?" said Maya. "What's the great deal in it?"

He looked at her, eyes narrowed. "Listen to me first. Let me complete."

"Okay okay," said Maya.

"At home, he felt upset, and came over to office. As he went to Srideviji's office, she said, 'Good morning, Anil. Happy birthday!'

"Anilji felt better that at least someone had remembered. Anilji worked till afternoon until Srideviji knocked at his door and said, 'It's such a wonderful day, the weather is awesome, and it's your birthday. Let's go out for lunch.'

"Anilji was elated, 'Wow, that's the best thing I've heard today. Let's go!'

"They went to a private little restaurant, got drunk and enjoyed their food. On the way back to the office, Srideviji said, 'We shouldn't go to the office on such a beautiful day, should we?'

"Anilji agreed, 'No, I guess not.'

"Srideviji said, 'Let's go to my flat. Nobody's there today. Let's have a memorable time on your birthday.'

"After arriving at her flat, she smiled and said, 'Anil, would you mind if I go to the bedroom and slip into something more comfortable?'

"Anilji excitedly replied, 'Of course!'

"Srideviji went into the bedroom, and in about few minutes, she returned. You can guess what present she gave him, and what happened after that," Raju said to Maya. He sipped his cold drink with a straw.

Maya's mouth was open and her hand covered her mouth.

"What? Really?" she asked, shocked.

"Really. He himself told me that. Do you know what really happened? In about a few minutes, Srideviji came out carrying a huge birthday cake followed by his wife, children and dozens of their friends from Kaizen, all singing 'Happy birthday...'! And he just sat there on the couch...*nirvastra!*"

Maya hit Raju with her hand.

"What!" Maya laughed crazily.

Raju was glad he had made her laugh. That day she laughed non-stop for long, like a child. People looked at her but she was unstoppable.

"Let's come to a serious point," she said, after she was able to control her laughter.

"Let's not get serious, and especially you," said Raju. "You look so beautiful when you are happy. You should always smile."

She blushed, her eyes on the table.

"Listen to me, please," she insisted, and he nodded.

"Okay, speak," he said. He looked into her eyes.

"I know you make good money out of the job. But do you have any plans about getting promoted or no?" she taunted, smiling.

"Miss Maya Kaushal, if it's like this then let me tell you, I'll become Business Head before you," Raju declared.

She laughed more vigorously this time. The motel manager looked at her from the corner of his eye.

She gathered herself and said, "It's good to have lofty dreams dear, but tell me, I'm serious. You should strive towards getting a promotion."

"I am thinking about it," he said.

"Then start working on it as the new month begins. You can be promoted the next month then if you are able to make 1200 sales. If...okay if!"

"I can, and in this month itself," he said. He passed a mischievous smile this time. "But I need your help."

"I'm always there for you. Just tell me what can I do for you?" she said seriously.

"There had been a slight change in criteria, right?" he asked.

"Yes. Earlier a salesman used to get fifteen percent of his sales and others had a fixed salary. It's the same as earlier, but a Manager, Senior Manager and Business Heads will get two percent commission on group sales along with their fixed salary. Earlier it was one percent," she replied.

"Means, for my every sale, you'll earn something extra?"

She nodded.

"How many sales do you have for the current month?"

"I have earned 7200 sales, and I am expecting it to reach 7500 by the time I submit them."

"Good. The promotion and contacts have increased your sales to good numbers," he said.

"All thanks to you," she smiled, while adjusting her hair.

"What will you get if you give your sales to company?"

"My salary, obviously! Why are you asking such illogical questions, ask some dillogical ones?"

They both laughed.

"Just salary, or, anything else as well?" he enquired, mischievously once more.

"No. But why?" she was curious as to where the conversation was headed.

"Look, your sales are likely to reach 7500, right?"

"Right."

"Give your 6500 sales to company."

"And the remaining 1000?" she wondered.

Raju smiled.

"What?" she asked again.

Looking at the ceiling, he sighed. "Me."

Maya looked at him, expressionless.

He explained. "My sales are 300 right now. If you give me your 1000 sales, my sales will cross the 1200 benchmark and I will be promoted. I'll become permanent this month. When the company will send my salary to my account, I'll return the money for the 1000 sales. So, you don't lose anything and I also get promoted. How's the idea?"

A smile lit up Maya's face. "Great!"

"And you forget that along with your salary and money for those one thousand sales," he said, "you get two percent commission as well from the company. But if you don't give your sales to me, neither will I be promoted nor will you get any commission."

She listened, mouth agape. He winked at her.

"Oh yes!" she exclaimed. "So much at one go! You're a genius, really."

She held Raju's hand and kissed it in excitement. But soon she realized what she had just done. She lowered her eyes and looked down with a smile on her face. He didn't spoil the atmosphere and ambience and responded with a warm smile.

Once again Raju wrote two identical letters, and sent one to Baba and one to Sanjay. In those letters he wrote:

Aadarniya Baba / Sanjay,

I wish for your wellbeing, and hope all you people are doing well.

I know you all have many complaints. It's been two years and I have not met you. I didn't even show up when grandfather died. I don't have words to apologize, but if you trust me, with all my humble devotion I prayed for his soul to find purpose. I also agree that in the last few months, I have not even written regularly. But now, difficult times for us have passed.

Your son has been promoted, and he has become a permanent employee of a very good company here in Bambai. Now he is well-established to take on his responsibilities and set you people free from yours. He earns well and thinks it will be more than sufficient for our family.

I would have loved to bring you here myself, Baba, but success brings responsibilities with it, so I won't be able to come myself and I really feel bad. But I will send one of my juniors to receive all of you.

Baba, please, start packing your bags.

I'll send my junior to Dhaneri on the fifteenth of the next month. His name is Johnny and he'll bring you to me. Don't worry and be comfortable with him. He is very trustworthy and will take care of you throughout the journey. And Sanjay, you too have to come. No excuses!

For years I have been running away, but not now. We will all live together here in Bambai. I can't live without you people anymore. Please come soon! I'm dying to see you all; I'm dying to see my family!

With all love and respect,

Your bholu son / bro,
Raju

Next month, Raju sent Johnny to Dhaneri, and his family including Sanjay came with him. They had no control over their emotions when they met Raju after two long years. Granny cried a lot that day.

Why do people cry during times of happiness? Maybe she was missing his grandfather, he thought.

Baba patted his back in appreciation of his success. Sanjay couldn't do anything as he was carrying the luggage! They all were so happy to be together once again.

Raju took two days off from the office and showed them around Bombay.

Granny seemed terrified by the city's crowds and high prices. She asked him how he managed in such an expensive city. Raju replied he earned a lot now. She was shocked to hear the amount while his father felt very proud.

Usha and Maya also came to meet them. His parents liked both of them, as both the ladies tried their best to impress his family. Sanjay asked Raju to tell him openly if he had any plans with either of the two. Raju explained to Sanjay and his family that they were just his colleagues. But was it really so?

Raju's life changed after his family came to Bombay. Morning and evening meals were eaten at home and Granny would wake him gently every day. He loved to listen to Baba's stories of different experiences in the field and Sanjay's constant teasing about Usha and Maya. Raju started loving his life all over again.

"One for you and the other for me. If not you, then I am interested in them. Any of the two will do for me," Sanjay often pulled his leg. "You just tell me which one you like. I'll leave her and try my luck with the other."

In office, he had a team to manage and he was a boss to six people. The 'good morning, sir' at the start of each day was pleasing to his ears.

But Raju was not satisfied. Having tasted success once, he was enchanted. One evening he invited Usha and Maya for dinner at the same motel, and they planned a promotion for Maya as they had done the previous time. The following month, she was promoted, and next to that month, Raju was promoted as well.

Maya was Manager now and Raju had become Sales Officer. Soon they met over dinner once more and they planned another promotion for Maya, followed by him. So in the following few months' time, he was Manager at Kaizen Internationals and Maya was Senior Manager.

People were in awe of their success. They were breaking old records and making new ones. With new records, they were making very good money as well. People started approaching them and showing much more respect. The other employees found an easy way to climb – walk with people who are already climbing up the ladder.

Their contacts list was getting longer by the day, and Kaizen Internationals was earning extremely good profits. Sridevi presented Raju and Maya a car each. His first car.

"As long as you are with Kaizen," Sridevi said.

Sanjay had already left for Dhaneri. Baba was happy for his success. And Granny had never experienced a car ride. For her, it was a dream come true. In fact, she had never even dreamt of owning something as big as a car.

"Only people with black money own such luxuries. I hope you are not doing anything unethical," warned Granny as they got back from a drive.

"Raju..." Maya screamed. She ran towards him and hugged him.

The evening he had won car from Sridevi, Maya called Raju and Usha to the motel. He assumed it was going to be one of their usual meetings, but he realized it was something else.

Maya was crying in his arms. He didn't know what had happened. People began staring at them. Hesitant, Raju made Maya release him and while he kept his hand on her head, he asked, "What happened?"

Usha was with him, surprised and jealous to see Maya in his arms.

"What happened?" he asked again, politely. But Maya didn't respond. Instead she cried louder.

Usha looked at Maya, her eyes red. "If you'll not tell us, how will we to help you?" she said rudely.

Maya continued to cry. Raju held her hand and said, "Maya!"

She looked at him. She came close and hugged him again. He tried to console her. Usha giggled, "Try to hold your breath, Maya, but can you really hold it?" She laughed at her own joke.

"My father died," finally Maya revealed.

The expressions on Usha's face changed abruptly. She spoke after a brief silence. "Then what are you doing here? You should go home."

Raju remained silent.

"I am just about to leave. Needed to inform you people so…" Maya sobbed.

Usha tried to gather words.

"Cry as much as you want to Maya, but just here. Once you stop crying, then don't start again, because there is someone who needs you…your mother. Don't cry in front of her," Raju broke his silence after a long time.

She was still hugging him. Usha rubbed her back and asked her to control herself, but Maya was difficult to handle. Raju gave her a glass of water.

"I need to go," Maya murmured after awhile.

"Okay," Usha said softly.

Understanding the loss, Raju simply nodded.

"These are my sales for this month. Keep it with you. I might take some time to return." Maya handed over her documents to Raju and left.

"Would you like to have something?" asked Usha.

He didn't answer. She asked again.

"No," he replied. "You?"

"Yes."

"What?"

"You."

"What?" he asked, shocked.

"Oh sorry. Just a slip of tongue. I mean whatever you want." She had hidden her feelings again that day.

He ordered one soup for Usha. "I'll have dinner at home with Baba," he justified as he didn't order anything for himself.

"Usha," said Raju.

"Hmm?"

"Have you ever lost a loved one?" he asked.

"No."

"So don't ever behave the way you did today." He sighed. "It hurts!" His face turned ashen.

"You okay?" Usha placed her hand on his. "I'm sorry, but I didn't know that Maya had lost her dad," she said defensively. "But why are you so serious?"

"Because I had lost someone too, years ago."

He still sat silent. A wild thought came to him as he wondered what he'd do the day Baba...His throat turned dry. He had lost Maa at an early age. He couldn't afford to lose Baba as well. He gulped down a glass of water and composed himself, because he knew it was not happening to him. At least not now!

"May I ask you something?" asked Usha.

"No," he said.

Usha didn't persist. Maybe she understood. She had her soup in silence and once she was done, he asked her, "Should I drop you home, or you'll go by yourself?"

"Yes, please. To your home."

"I hope it's not a slip tongue this time."

"No, it's not," she said, "I want to meet Baba."

"Uncle, don't you think Granny needs someone for assistance? She's old now. Aren't you people in search of a bride for our Manager?" Usha asked Baba over dinner, glancing at Raju from the corner of her eye.

Raju looked at her in shock.

Holy hell!

"It's difficult to find good girls with moral values these days, beta. Where will we find a girl like you?" joked Granny.

"I'm waiting for a green signal, Ammaji. My luggage is ready," Usha giggled.

She didn't talk to Maya nicely today, but the moment we reached home Usha went directly to the kitchen to help Granny and now this...What was she up to today? Raju wondered.

Looking at Usha, Raju said, "I'm just twenty-five. And I have no plans to marry."

Raju and Usha had been working hard together. His next aim was the post of Business Head and an office he had dreamt of the day he had entered Sridevi's office.

The criteria to become a Business Head were 100,000 sales for one month with a hundred or more members working under you. Raju and Maya had done some brilliant work in the past few months, so many people wanted to work under him, and as a result, he had more than hundred-and-fifty members under him which played out to be a turner for him during his last days at Kaizen Internationals.

Raju was promoted once again, and he had become a Senior Manager. Unfortunately, Maya was not there with him, and he couldn't say anything to the others, but he missed her.

Usha had proposed to him the night she had stayed at his house.

"I don't feel good when Maya comes close to you. I feel jealous! I'm really waiting for a green signal," she had said but Raju had not answered her. His entire focus was on one thing – sales.

Managing 100,000 sales in one month was very difficult. There were a very few people who had managed to do it till now. In India, there were only twelve people, and they had taken many years to achieve that level. The least time taken was by Sridevi – seven years. Raju was still two months short of completing two years. He realized he lacked experience that was important, but he had feasible plans. But his plans would have shaken the foundations of the company, if he had gone through with them.

After giving it a serious thought, he decided to corrupt the entire workforce at Kaizen Internationals.

Raju invited Usha for dinner and handed her a document.

"What is this?" questioned Usha.

"Read it," replied Raju.

She read the document. It was a ten page long non-disclosure agreement. She read the last page – Appendix – aloud in confusion.

1. The Donor will obey any instructions given by The Acceptor.
2. The Donor will agree to any professional activity deemed fit and increase sales for the term.
3. He/she will do so eagerly and without hesitation.
4. The Donor will ensure he/she achieves a minimum of eight hours of sleep a night to be exhaust free on field and give his/her best.
5. The Donor will eat regularly to maintain his/her health and well-being.
6. The Donor will wear proper professional clothing and maintain professional looks.
7. The Donor shall have a proper haircut and shave on time, if male.
8. The Donor will not drink to excess, take recreational drugs, or put himself/herself in any unnecessary danger.
9. The Donor will conduct himself/herself in a respectful and modest manner at all times on field. He/she must recognize that his/her behavior is a direct reflection on the sales and the company.

"What is this for?" asked a confused Usha. "I can arrange sales without this. I have been doing it for such a long time."

"Usha, the previous month, on your advice I used all of Maya's sales and got a promotion. Since the past one year you have helped me and Maya a great deal in arranging sales and promoting us. You were a receptionist when I joined, Maya a Sales In-charge and I was a to-be-a-salesman. Not even a salesman then. Today I and Maya are Senior Managers, and what are you? You are still a receptionist," Raju said.

Usha looked at him. I did it for you, her eyes said.

He continued, "Once you said that I have made Maya. I am responsible for her promotion and her success. But the reality is that without thinking of yourself, and being unselfish and kind, you did it for us. You are responsible for our good."

"Dear…" she held his hand.

"Let me speak, Usha," he said, "I know you did it because you have feelings for me, but I don't have answers for you, dear. I am deeply immersed in this work, and I don't understand relationships."

Usha continued to look at him.

He took a deep sigh. "I am not good at them."

A picture of Guddi crossed his mind.

"I am very week at relationships." He repeated.

"Why are you saying all this today?" asked Usha.

"Because I too want to think about something else. I too want to see beauty, I too want to spend some good times, and I too want to live a simple life. In the end – I too am human."

"Then why don't you? Who is stopping you?"

"No one."

"Then what are you in search of, dear?"

She looked surprised. "You have already accomplished so much in life. You are almost a Business Head. You have a very good job, you have two cars, you have a lot of money, and you have your family with you. In this country, you are a very rich man on many grounds and happy too."

"But none of that gives me peace, Usha," he said, in a very low tone.

For first time in Raju's life, after Sanjay, he shared his emotions with someone. He knew that Usha liked him, but this was the first time he was opening up to her.

"All a young man needs is a young woman to love and be loved. It's been a while since I've expressed my feelings to you. I thought you'll respond to me the way you feel, but you've never told me anything," said Usha.

"The matters of the heart understand only one language – feelings. Why do you love me Usha?" he asked.

"Because I simply do. Remember that where your heart is, there lies peace for you. You give me your heart, I'll bring you peace."

I'm getting emotional and she's getting patriotic. 'You give me blood, I'll give you freedom. A Subhash Chandra Bose fan!

He said nothing.

"I want to marry you." Usha broke the silence a few minutes later. "And want to live with you. I know that you have dreams to accomplish, and you are born to win your karma, but trust me dear, I love you very much."

Raju's one hand was holding a spoon and his eyes were on the food. However, he paused, and looked at her before saying, "I have a dream to pursue and a journey to complete, Usha. And even if somehow we get married, our life wouldn't be what you may be dreaming of. Initially we'll be a married couple with a lot of happiness. We'll take some time and in that time we'll get to know each other. Some more time will pass, and we'll understand each other better."

He continued, "Today I am on a path to somewhere, but once I get married it will change and with it, my pursuits of life too will change. Few years later, maybe one, two, or three, you'll see a change in me, but you'll ignore it trying to be an understanding partner. Few more years will pass, and you'll observe continuous changes in me, that will be natural. A day will arrive when you'll be unhappy to see me. You'll feel, it was you who interrupted my pursuit. But you will love me, and I will love you in return. I'll never say anything because I've been its victim once and I know what love demands, so I won't blame you ever. But, there will be times when I'll miss the journey I am on now. And I'll think about how it would have been, had I discovered it."

Usha seemed hurt.

Raju continued, "Then, after many years, you'll be fed up of my attitude, and we'll fight. In rage, you'll shout and scream at me, and will yell at me to go and complete my abandoned journey, but by then, it will be too late."

Usha looked at him, numb. Her dreams were crumbling in front of her.

"We'll have a life, and we'll have a responsibility. I'd never be able to do it then, and hence, we both will live a life of regret," he explained.

Usha had stopped eating.

"We've been together for such a long time. Don't you feel anything for me?" she choked.

"Your heart reveals the pureness of your love. And only feelings can understand the matters of the heart. If you want to know what my heart speaks of you Usha, don't ask, feel! Feelings will delineate and define," he said.

"Sometimes you talk like a wise man," said Usha, looking down and playing nervously with her fingernails.

"Only sometimes, when the feelings within me start flowing. I have learnt it from someone." He thought of Sanjay and continued, "Usha, please accept this dear, that loving someone is natural, but to live with a person that resides in your heart is a strategy created by your own mind. The existence of love is for a purpose. Love was born so that through its power, it could refine the soul of the human and bring a change in them for the world to change for the better. And that's what I mean by feelings."

He smiled at her. "The matters of the heart understand only the law of nature, and that is to let whatever is happening happen. Be it whatever, good or bad, it will end in good, always. Everything ends with good, and it's the law of nature."

"What keeps you inspired not to live a normal human life and work so hard?" she half-smiled.

"Desire," Raju answered. "Desire itself is an inspiration."

He resumed eating his food and murmured, "I might need to sell my new car in order to accomplish my dream."

Usha heard his words.

"New car? For Business Head?" She was shocked.

Usha realized he was really crazy. He was ready to sell his new car for a single promotion.

"Yes. And for that I need your help." He came directly to the point.

He said, "You have everybody's contacts as you deal with all the paperwork. They get job letters from you and you have everybody's information, and everybody knows you well. I want you to target members of other groups other than mine. There are hundreds of employees in this office. You have to find some ambitious ones who want more. The ambitious ones are to be targeted."

"What do I need to do?" she enquired.

The topic coolly shifted from emotions.

"What you had been doing till now. Plus this contract," he answered.

"I can do without it. Why this?"

"I know you can. But I don't want to shake the foundations of Kaizen once I leave after becoming Business Head. I don't want people to talk. This contract will bind them to keep things between the three of us – you, me and the person who gives us the sales. And guess what?"

"What?"

"People will easily come, because they'll get six times the money of the original price. To manage the money, I need to sell my new car. Even if they don't work for the next six months, they'll still be able to live well and eat well."

Usha nodded, taking a gulp, and as usual, she agreed.

Usha was smart, as well as beautiful. She knew how to get work done. At least this she had learnt from Raju in these years. She told the Donors that Raju was the Acceptor and then nobody dared to refuse. And so, she got the contract signed from different members of different groups.

Raju met them personally, one by one, and gave them part of the money in advance, as per terms of the contract, and it kept them enthusiastic on the field. He kept meeting them when possible and kept inspiring them to elevate the sales.

In that entire month, there was not a single day when he reached home before midnight or had all of his meals for the day. To the Donors he had given strict instructions about health and sleep, but he himself would skip one or the other meal, and never got enough sleep in thirty days. After all, the Donors were the ones who had to face the clients and earn on the field. He just had to manage them.

Though they were not members of his group, nor was he their senior, he managed them well and they all worked together for his promotion.

One month finally passed. According to the contract, the Donors gave him their sales a day before the last day of a contract term, and he rewarded them with the sum of six times the original price.

Maya had just returned after a period of two months and so much had changed in her absence. Raju was standing on the stage in the company's auditorium with Sridevi and people were applauding. After all, he was to make history at Kaizen Internationals. He had become the first Business Head under Sridevi. With this history, he had made one more.

He returned the sales of half of the people who had signed the contract and they were promoted with him. There were so many promotions on one day. For Sridevi, it was a miracle; but for him, it came after a lot of blood and sweat.

The mother company gave Raju an option to select a territory anywhere in India, and Sridevi had given him a car permanently as a farewell present. Raju met Usha and Maya one last time, and told them that he had no plans to get married, because he had a lot to do. In fact, his journey had just started. He hoped they understood!

*H*e never led a life of regret, but when Raju was leaving Kaizen, he regretted the fact that he had corrupted the workforce of an organization that he had served for two years. Sridevi would never realize how Raju did in two years what took her seven.

Corrupting the entire workforce at the Bombay office, Raju migrated to Delhi. He named his branch 'KBC' which marketed for GrowingWings Group.

He purchased one luxurious apartment in one of the posh colonies in the city. The office was a forty-five minute drive from his apartment. He decided that the office timings were to be from ten in the morning to eight in the evening and gave a handsome salary to his employees. There were no temporary members in his company and everyone was treated equally. And before he started working in his branch, he recollected all he had done in the past to reach the level of a Business Head, in order to plan the platform for his own employees.

The first thing he had done when he was at Kaizen on a week off was that he made a report. In that report he wrote some salient points – why employees took so much time to become permanent, and why do they leave. First he made a report, and then a plan. He implemented it stepwise and it worked. When you implement your plans, they mostly fail; but when you implement them step-wise, they work out. The same happened with him. Most of the first timers used to leave their job at Kaizen, because they couldn't manage the sales, and as salary was not fixed they couldn't manage to live on the amount they earned. So what he did was, he gave his sales to members in his group so that they'd stick to the company, and he managed sales for himself with the help of Usha and Maya. He even gave his sales to his juniors in order to get them promoted soon. Once they were promoted, they had their own group and their salaries were fixed, so he didn't need to give them his sales anymore, and the increasing group was obviously a plus point. His juniors got promoted early in this manner. They all had big groups and it made it easy for him to hit his criteria as the workforce was always good. Parties, Maya's promotion, dinners at the motel – every single penny spent was all planned. Maya was dynamic and enthusiastic about work. He needed a senior above him on good terms, so, before his promotion, he made her get promoted every time and that made his own senior indebted to him. He was creating a bridge for himself to achieve his dreams. Maya had a better workforce than his, so later she could have helped him a great deal. Usha brought sales from members of other groups;they did get money from him, but their sales, according to the company's records were always low and his high. He was honoured by everyone and got promotions early. At last he had to draw up the contract to keep his reputation intact in the eyes of the senior officers of the company.

Things were not much different at his own office at KBC than Kaizen Internationals. It was similar to a great extent on the face of it, but the principles were different. Salespersons were already permanent. They had no pressure or fear. He gave them respect and inspired them every morning by sharing new things with them that he had discovered while he was at their position. Many a times, he threw parties and all the people in all positions were invited. He even listened to their personal problems, if some were disturbed, and helped them in any way he could. It all inspired them, keeping them dedicated towards their work.

Once his business started to take shape, he imported a brand new BMW from Germany for his parents. Eventually, as his tours and drives had increased a lot with responsibilities, he also imported a Range Rover from the United States for himself. After all, SUVs are comfortable for long trips!

Unlike Kaizen, where everyone was busy managing sales themselves and their promotions, in KBC people helped each other with sales and promotions. They didn't compete with each other. It resulted in miracles and his juniors broke the record Raju had created once.

Five people became Business Heads on KBC's first birthday. Everyone was shocked. He was the first Business Head under any daughter company in twenty-six nations where GrowingWings Group was based. The Chairman and CEO were astounded.

The new Business Heads were honoured well and when they were asked the territory they would like to work in, Delhi was the answer. They didn't want to start their own business; they wanted to work under Raju. It was against the company's policy, but the new Business Heads stuck to it. The CEO of GrowingWings Group, Mr Tom Alter came to India to resolve the problem. Raju made arrangements for Tom's stay at Hyatt Regency, Delhi. They met each other for the first time and both were impressed with each other's personalities.

When asked why they didn't want to start their own businesses under GrowingWings Group, the new Business Heads said, "We want to work with KBC."

The CEO tried to explain that Raju was a Business Head and so were they; one Business Head cannot work under the other. But the new Business Heads were persistent. And then was history created at GrowingWings Group once more, not only in India this time, but all across the globe.

"We'll work as Business Heads in KBC and you can promote Raju sir to the next level," one of the newly formed Business Heads said, and then CEO realized that time had come for first ever Country Head at GrowingWings Group.

The CEO talked to the Chairman and Raju was declared Country Head, but not only in India, in fact in all the twenty-six countries where GrowingWings Group was working. Was this promotion, too, planned by Raju? Or, had he really merited it? Only this fox knew!

His new job was to go to every country and work on the reasons why other countries had not been able to create even a single Country Head in so many years.

In short: Raju had become the boss of more than 90,000 employees and more than 600 Business Heads in twenty-six nations.

When we hear, we just don't give a damn; when we listen, we hardly pay heed; and when we read, we just portray; but when we feel – only then we reveal. So just imagine, and you'll feel something.

Imagine…

…that this is the biggest day of your life. You are getting promoted as Country Head of a multinational company. You are sitting in the back seat of your Range Rover. Your chauffer is driving the car and you are going to the venue where you are to be honoured as Country Head of twenty-six countries.

...that you are wearing an Armani suit and a Rolex wrist watch. One expensive Mont Blanc is in your pocket. Your black shoes are costlier than your pen and shine brighter than a star. You are all covered with most luxurious brands in the world. There are many people in this country who own a house that is equivalent in worth to your pen, wrist watch, shoes, or suit that you are wearing.

...that sitting in your Range Rover you see people walking outside, and you notice some poor children selling things for a living. At one traffic signal your car stops as the light turns red, one small untidy girl, wearing dirty clothes selling red heart-shaped balloons approaches you. By then the traffic signal turns green and your car moves ahead towards the venue. But that poor little girl with the red balloons on the street is still in your head. She reminds you of your times on the street and you remember the times of your childhood.

...that you were born in a very small village of an under developed country, without many facilities, and spent your childhood there. Wearing shorts, you used to play gulli-danda, kanche and fly kites during your childhood days. You used to live in a hut and your mother used to cook food at the hearth. You grew up playing all day with your friends, one among them a girl. You and all your friends used to wave your hands in the air and scream, helicopter-bye-helicopter-bye in excitement when a helicopter would pass overhead. And by the time you reached the last days of your schooling, you left the city. You went out in search of a living and worked hard. A year later, you see the girl you loved once, with all your true feelings. You fell for your love once more and this time you proposed to her.

She refused and then you turned crazy. One friend, like an angel, arrived in your life and helped you come out of that insane world. You became a workaholic. Once again you didn't think of anyone. Don't know from whom you are running. Your parents, the girl you loved, friends, the society, this world, or, from yourself?

...that this is a day when you are being honoured as the very first person to achieve a certain position in twenty-six countries. Ahead of your car is a Mercedes in which other officials are sitting. A chauffer-driven BMW is following your car in which your father, grandmother and Sanjay are sitting. And in between is your Range Rover in which you are sitting along with the CEO of the mother company.

...you reach the venue. There are many people standing to receive you. Few press people wants to talk to you, but you enter the hotel. After a while you see yourself sitting on the stage with the CEO. You see all the Business Heads and other Managers of different companies giving you a standing ovation. Many Business Heads have even travelled from other countries to be present at your promotion ceremony, and basically, to see a man who gives birth to miracles. Your ex-boss is the first person to speak in your honour and then it is the CEO who honors you with a trophy, a contract, and a cheque. You stand beside the CEO and look at the guests. You see them applauding for you. You look at your parents. They had always dreamt of making you a great person and sacrificed their big dreams for your small ones. But their biggest dream has come true today, so they are smiling and clapping.

...that the stage you are standing on faces hundreds of guests who are sitting in different groups at one side, and

the media on the other. Behind you is a big digital screen in which your photograph and name with the subtitle 'World's first Country Head at GrowingWings Group' flashes every now and then. The entire room is decorated with different beautiful fresh flowers of different colors and there is a buffet with dishes from all over the world. Behind the buffet stalls stand stewards, erect as soldiers standing at the front, and a few stewardesses are serving snacks and drinks to the guests.

...that people are enjoying the moment. You receive your trophy and other awards. The CEO gives the credit to your parents for your success and there are tears in your parents' eyes.

...that you have made your parents proud!

...that you are holding the mike and looking around at the different people. You observe one out of many beautiful ladies in that room – a girl you had loved once, twice, or any number of times. But you have loved her with all your true feelings. She is wearing a sari. Her hair tied. Her skin glowing. A perfect combination of beauty and simplicity. She watches you. Your eyes meet with hers and she looks down. You have loved her with all your true feelings and planned your entire life around her. You gaze at her continuously. Your love for her is the greatest and for eternity. Suddenly, you see her holding a tray full of snacks that she is serving to the different guests.

...that she is a stewardess there!

...that you see her going to every person, and she smiles asking if they would like to have the snacks. Some people are being served and some refuse. Some people are focussed

on you and some are looking at her malevolently. Standing there you observe people looking at her and giggling among themselves. She goes to you parents. Your father takes a snack, smiles and looks at you again. She smiles back at him and heads to your brother. Your brother makes a face as he sees her, behaves as if he never knew her, looks at you and smiles. For two seconds, the expression of the girl you truly love changes, but soon she composes herself, and walks ahead with the same enthusiasm and smile on her face. You notice your brother's brother has turned rich and your brother has turned egoistic.

...that soon you realize while you have been looking at your love, people have been looking at you, waiting for your speech. But can you really speak now? Do you have the strength to utter even a single word?

...that for a woman, her honour is the greatest and most valuable trinket she possesses, but your love has lost it. It's not that she doesn't know what your brother did to her, or, she did not notice that people were talking about her. She knows it all! The thing is, she is accustomed to humiliation now, and, under that fake smile is deep pain, and thirst for respect.

These were just a few moments of his life, a life which he had lived and moments through which he had passed. None of the milestones in history have been achieved by anyone alone. The biggest battles, the greatest monuments, the greatest discoveries, and sagas have been brought about by different forces which joined together. Achievers start their journeys alone but end with many around them.

Success never comes easy. You are tested on the scale of difficulties. The bigger the success, the higher the difficulty level of your testing times. Raju knew it, because he was a person who had been tested on a very tough scale. When we follow our heart, we always tend towards improvisation, and so we transform ourselves from raw material like coal, into a precious diamond. He was forced into depression for three years, but he won, and he came out with flying colours. People quit when they are about to accomplish their dreams. Though it happens every day and nature screams every morning to tell everyone that, they never realize that the darkest hour of the night comes just before the dawn. For him too, a time had come. Was it the darkest hour or the dawn, he didn't know.

At his award ceremony in the hotel, Sanjay had not behaved well with Guddi, and people didn't show her respect. And all that happened in front of Raju. What was he doing? Watching all that! His eyes were moist when he stood on the stage, and people applauded him. People thought it was because of success he had gained that his eyes were wet, but only he knew it was because of his failure. He had lost love, peace, and a lot more to stand there above everyone. And he had lost a lot more than that. He was standing there holding a trophy, but he had lost the biggest thing in life.

That was the first time Raju got an opportunity to speak out his heart, but there was a bit more to be done.

He wanted to scream and tell everybody his success story, his story of hardship and everything he had to go through to reach the point he was at. He wanted people to applaud and scream his name louder. He wanted to prove to everybody that he was a unique gem.

But how could he tell everybody that there have been people who are interested only in earning money, and focusing only on honour? They never tried anything out of the box. They forgot that there were many ways to achieve your goals, not just one. They forgot it's a path function, and not a point function. Then they became so accustomed to living and working in that manner, that they were never able to discover themselves.

How could he tell them that your thinking becomes your actions, and your actions become your destiny? Have you ever seen a child? He is always happy, unaware of any pain. Why? Because he saves for good times. He saves in his piggy bank just as elders save in their banks. But a child saves for his happiness – for his birthday, a pen, a bag, a cycle, or a toy...so he stays happy. And elders save for difficult times, so difficult times haunt them frequently. It's not that pain chooses us, or hard moments come to us, but it's we who invite them, by dreaming of them even before they arrive.

He wanted to deliver, but how could he. We are born to manifest the glory of every single dream of ours. But don't know what happens to humankind. As it grows, instead of being more daring and winning, it fears and loses.

How could he possibly tell this to his audience, that if you want to be a dominating person, in your personal or professional life, the first thing you should do is, stop being dominated yourself.

He wanted to say all this. He wanted to be a motivational speaker for a day, and he wanted to be an example for others. He wanted them to hear him. He wanted to impress them a bit more, but all he could do was, as people waited for him to speak, sit down...numb.

He sat on the floor of the stage.

He was left to do with nothing after watching those moments. How could he really open up when those moments had broken his honour and scattered it into many pieces!?

He came out and drove back home.

Along with his family, the people at the ceremony were surprised at his strange behaviour, but that day, he had more pressing things to focus upon, so he didn't give a damn. Raju's heart seemed to have undergone a rebirth after years!

"Why didn't you tell me earlier?" scowled Raju.

"I couldn't," defended Sanjay. "Maa was dead, Raju! Baba had none other than you. And she was responsible for your mental breakdown." Sanjay's words choked. "I didn't want to lose you again for another three years. I did it for us."

"Guddi was not responsible for my mental breakdown, Bhaiji." Raju took a deep breath. "I took it the wrong way. She simply never ever loved. Just the way I didn't love Usha or Maya. It's a feeling. You can't force it."

It was midnight. Everyone was asleep in their rooms. Sanjay and Raju lay on the bed in Raju's room. Raju had not talked to anyone after coming back from the event. He directly came to his room. Sanjay managed to convince Baba that everything was fine and made him go to sleep after dinner, while he came to Raju's room.

"I know it's difficult to fight feelings, but I was afraid," said Sanjay.

"Whatever," said Raju. "Now you can tell me all the details?"

Sanjay switched on bed light. "On one condition."

"Now what?" asked an irritated Raju.

"I'm hungry. Join me for something to eat."

"Means you want to force me to eat?" Raju rolled his eyes.

Sanjay smiled. Raju nodded.

"Sanjay, let's take him to Dr Mishra," said Granny. "Or put some sense in him."

"Ammaji," said Raju.

"No," she said. "That girl will not become the daughter-in-law of my house."

Raju had dropped a nuclear bomb on his family with the news the next day that he wanted to marry Guddi – someone who had run away once, married someone from a different caste against her parent's wishes, was a separated woman, and had a daughter as well. Raju had forgotten he had his family to convince. Graveness overshadowed his house. His father showed his displeasure with a few words, but his grandmother did what women are best at. She cried a lot!

"It's your call, bro. But you should be careful. She is married, has a baby, and we live in an undemocratic society of a so-called democratic country," Sanjay said. "You need to learn how to be selective in your actions. This is a power everyone must cultivate."

"But Sanjay..." Raju said, "At least you should understand me, man."

"No." Granny threatened Raju. "I'll drink poison if you take any wrong step."

Raju kept shut. He couldn't open his mouth now.

Though Raju wanted to speak a lot in his defense, he couldn't. He couldn't explain to them one simple thing that love is not an act to cultivate the mind or nurture thoughts, it is a feeling that is spontaneous and eternal. Love is not the exclusive privilege of the brainy or dumb. There is, there has been, there will be a certain group of people whom this lovely feeling of love visits. It's made up of all those who've consciously chosen their calling and who always listen to their heart. It may include the rich or poor, married or unmarried, young or old, man or woman. He couldn't explain to them that for people who are in love, life becomes one continuous adventure as long as they manage to keep discovering new feelings. Difficulties and setbacks never quell their curiosity. Utter happiness emits from every single step they take in love. Whatever love is, it definitely is the sweetest mystery that I, or anyone else will ever get to taste.

Every person has a goal in his life, a destination where he dreams his journey to end. And if he runs after that destination, takes any path and becomes insane to reach his goal, it is utterly justified. But if someone is running here and there without any reason, without knowing why he is doing it, then that is utterly unjustified.

Throughout life, he worked hard to chase his dream, but found nothing. He felt weighed down by the obstacles, but he didn't stop. Raju struggled to continue chasing his dream as he fought destiny, which was often against him. He learnt that he was running after something that not even he was aware of. He realized neither he had Guddi with him nor happiness. He discovered that, years ago, in that pain and writhe for Guddi was more peace and satisfaction than winning promotions and making money. He realized that his life was aimless.

Living a life without a purpose is worthless, so he decided to give meaning to his life. Sole rejection turns even a swindler into an ascetic. Its shadow fell on him as well! He was abraded and exhausted, but he listened to his heart. It had told Raju to love the woman he had fallen in love with years ago. While he was in love, the sweet feeling educated him, and laws were imparted to him in an act which had no actions. But now he had decided to restart his life, and had done it well.

A few months passed. No one had talked about Guddi after the day Granny blackmailed him saying she'd give up her life. Raju tried hard to continue his life the way it had been going. He tried to immerse himself in work, but his mind couldn't win over his heart. Outside he was tough, but inside he burnt. He started skipping his meals. He stopped taking care of himself. He stayed lost over Guddi's thoughts, thinking what would have become of her. In the months that followed, his health deteriorated.

"Ammaji, I have not seen Baba since a few days. Where is he?" asked Raju one day.

"I sent him somewhere for some important work," answered Granny.

As he sat on a chair beside her to read a newspaper, he rubbed his hair. Granny looked at him, gloomily.

"Not going to office today?" she asked.

"No. Got a headache!"

Granny nodded.

"Raju, do you have any idea what my age is?" asked Granny.

"You are in your eighties, I suppose," said Raju, his eyes on the newspaper.

She smiled. "And yours?"

"Twenty-six," he replied.

"Say we both score a century." Granny continued to smile looking at Raju. He looked elsewhere. She continued, "For my remaining one silver jubilee, you have decided to give up your three jubilees?"

"I didn't get you, Ammaji," said a confused Raju. He looked at her now, putting the paper down.

Granny continued, "I am done with my life. This is my bonus time, my child. But for you, life has just started and you look so depressed. You seem like you are in your fifties and speak like a man in his eighties."

"It's nothing like that, Ammaji." Raju looked away.

"That is clearly visible, dear. Do you have plans to become a Devdas?" she asked.

"No." Raju was not at all interested. Guddi's topic was resurfacing after months. He picked up the newspaper again and dived into it.

"I want to talk to you, Bholu?" Granny used his nickname; it meant something serious was coming.

Raju folded the newspaper and placed it on the table again.

"Be open and frank with me, dear, because this is regarding all of us."

She dragged her chair closer. "Look, soon I'll be gone and then your Baba too, but you'll live; you'll live for us. We will be dead, yet we will live in you and you in your children later. That is the law of nature."

"Hmm." Raju nodded.

"What is more important, Raju, love or marriage?" she asked.

"For different people, the answer will be different."

"I'm asking you."

"To me, Ammaji, both are one and a same thing. I can't choose one over the other." He folded his hands. "To me, life is more important."

"That is not the answer, dear."

"Then, to me, I don't see marriage as the union of two people or families. I see marriage as union of two hearts. And two hearts unite only when there's love. Without love, nothing can exist. Not even a single relation. Not even marriage." Raju took a deep breath, his eyes closed. "You know Ammaji, there was a time when I ran away from everyone because I didn't want any pain in my life. I was a coward and didn't want to face the challenges of life. I thought a life of peace is more important, but can you really live all alone, all of your life, expecting peace to come to you?" He exhaled, opening his eyes, and continued, "You can't spend all of your life alone waiting for something you aren't sure of. You need someone to share your feelings and peace with. For me, that someone is Guddi with whom I wanted to go through the good and bad times of my life, but as I said I was a coward, and I kept running away." He sighed deeply.

"May I ask you something?" Granny looked at him in astonishment.

Raju nodded.

"What did you see in that girl?"

"Nothing!" he replied. "She is just a normal girl. I am abnormal. My heart is abnormal. So is every lover's. In love, we don't see, we just feel. That's why I said, love is a feeling."

"And what do you feel that you are so serious about her?"

"Everything good that exist in this universe, I feel all that for her," Raju said with a smile on his face. "You know, Ammaji, no matter what others feel or say about her, for me, whenever I talk of her, I see her, I think of her – I smile. I feel energetic and inspired. I feel like a king. Loving her gives me peace."

Lost in his world of love, Raju continued to speak. He didn't move an inch. Granny listened to him. She was moved by him. He had smiled after months, and that meant he was correct – Guddi was the one who could make him smile. Sitting there in front of him, Granny observed how that young mournful unhealthy boy who had looked old a few minutes ago looked young again. His body emitted happiness. Just then, when Raju was lost in his dream world, he felt a heavy tap on his shoulder. He was surprised to see Sanjay.

Sanjay went to Granny. "Raam raam, Ammaji," said Sanjay, touching her feet. Granny blessed him. Baba too had come.

Sanjay hugged Raju. "How are you?"

"Fine." Raju smiled. "Nice surprise."

"Get ready for a heart attack." Sanjay patted Raju's back.

"Sit," said Granny.

Everyone sat down. They looked at one another.

Granny looked at Baba. Baba looked at Sanjay. Raju looked at them, unaware of what was going on. He had been in a very bad mood for months and had not been in conversation with anyone. He decided to be a mute spectator.

"So, how was it?" asked Granny.

Sanjay smiled, closed his eyes and nodded. He looked at Raju once his eyes opened. Raju looked at him, expressionless.

"He was teaching me about love," said Granny, to Baba and Sanjay. "The boy is serious."

A servant arrived with a tray of water glasses. Sanjay took one glass. "Ahhh!" he exclaimed. "Really? What?"

"Nothing," said Raju. "Where were you, Baba?" He turned to Baba.

Baba, once again, looked at Sanjay. The servant had left by then.

"Have you ever heard of parents giving second birth to their children, Raju?" asked Sanjay.

"No." He asked, "Why does everybody sound so mysterious?"

"Baba..." Sanjay looked at Baba.

"Son, we have taken a decision..." Baba looked at Granny. "Why don't you tell him, Ammaji. You're the eldest in the family."

Granny smiled. "Bholu..."

Raju mentally prepared himself for things to come and listened patiently.

She continued. "Just a few minutes ago you said that you can't spend your life all alone...so we have found a match for you."

"Match...means...?" asked a confused Raju.

"Well, we feel that you shouldn't delay it any longer now. So, Ammaji sent me to Banda with your marriage proposal. The girl's side has agreed." Baba smiled, pointing towards Sanjay. "He too accompanied me. They are happy about this, and so are we."

Raju looked at Sanjay. He felt cheated. Raju looked at Baba. He felt hurt. Raju looked at Granny. He had been emotionally blackmailed. He couldn't respond. He swallowed a lump forming in his throat. "Why didn't you tell me?"

"We are following the tradition, Bholu," said Granny. "My parents chose a partner for me, we chose one for your baba, and now we are doing so for you."

"I know that, Ammaji," resisted Raju. "But that was a different time. And…" His face turned ashen, and heart pumped faster.

Love never dies a natural death. It dies because we don't know how to replenish its source. It dies of blindness and errors and betrayals. It dies of illness and wounds. It dies of weariness, of withering, of tarnishing. Granny observed, once again, the change in Raju. Just a few minutes had passed, but he had turned old again. He was turning older.

"You're not in your teens anymore, my child," said Granny. "Grow up." She frowned. "This tension of yours makes us weak."

Yet you don't understand. Yet you don't feel. Yet you don't change.

Raju's heart turned heavy. He looked down. He buried one of his fingernails deep into the skin around the wrist to divert his mind from emotional pain to physical pain. He felt helpless. His tear glands held an ocean in them, but couldn't release a single drop. Just then, Sanjay saw what Raju had been doing to his wrist. He rushed to him and grabbed his wrist. Raju hugged Sanjay. "Don't do this to me."

"We're just trying to help you, bro. As far as the doing part is concerned, you have to perform the major part." Sanjay held Raju back. "We went Banda to meet Guddi's parents, you moron! Now control yourself."

Raju's heart seized, his breath stopped and brain went blank. He turned to look at Granny.

"Can't ruin your three silver jubilees for my one," said Granny. "I sent your Baba to your Guddi's house, to her parents. Not someone else, Bholu." Granny smiled.

Raju looked at Baba, dazed.

"Yes Raju," said Baba, "Ammaji asked me to visit Guddi's parents a few days ago. We went there, half sure of how things would turn out, but unexpectedly, things went well. Her parents have agreed."

Raju held Sanjay's hand, tight. Sanjay clasped his tighter. Tears started to flow. And this time it wasn't a drop or two. Neither was it a drizzle. It was a heavy shower, with thunder and lightning. Raju ran to Granny and sat at her feet. He held her legs, embracing them, kept his head on her lap and the volcanic ocean of tears erupted. Granny caressed his hair. "Crazy! Totally crazy!" she cried.

"Okay now," interrupted Sanjay. "Time to laugh, Ammaji." He was standing with Baba. Baba held his shoulder.

Raju wiped his tears and nose, and came to Baba. He touched Baba's feet. Baba held him. "Today, my arms are your place, my son." Baba hugged Raju as Sanjay patted Raju's back.

"But how did you do it? I mean, there was no need to hide," said Raju to Sanjay.

"You two talk. I'll freshen up." Baba patted Raju's cheeks and left with Granny.

Raju hugged Sanjay again. "Thanks, Bhaiji."

"I'm straight, Raju," giggled Sanjay, "and you're getting married, so control yourself!"

Raju punched Sanjay on his chest.

"A walk?" asked Sanjay.

"Anything!" Raju smiled.

Sanjay was driving Raju to the hotel where Guddi worked. Sanjay had insisted Raju go alone, but seeing Raju nervous, Sanjay agreed to drive him there and wait in the car.

"Focus!" said Sanjay, as he drove through the streets of Delhi.

Raju nodded, his heartbeat increasing every minute as they approached the hotel.

"I've not met her, Raju." Sanjay took the conversation forward, "but she will be difficult to convince, I feel."

"I know. She is a very stubborn woman," said Raju. "I've known this since childhood. And I was not prepared for it initially, but now I am."

"Do you know what she said to her parents before running away?" asked Sanjay, exclaimed.

"What?"

"That you're not going to decide who I sleep with," Sanjay said.

"Did she?" Raju sat startled. "Who told you this?"

"Yes, she did. Her father said she was so against marrying someone she didn't know properly."

Raju didn't say anything. He just increased the speed of the air conditioner.

Sanjay continued, "In a way, she was wrong. Wasn't she?"

"And in a way," said Raju, "she wasn't."

"Now don't defend her."

"I'm not." Raju was serious. "Even I have my reservations about this practice. Parents' approval is fine, but do you see how, in most of the cases, girls are sent to her in-laws as if she is a burden. Her choice or viewpoint is insignificant. Leave choice, she is not even asked. The family meets the suitor, the family meets the family and the marriage is fixed. That's not all, the family looks at wealth, community, caste, and creed. The family scrutinizes the family the most and the suitor the least. Does someone's financial or social status define their virtue or compatibility?"

Sanjay laughed, as he drove. "Good Mr Lover, but mind you," said Sanjay, "her parents have agreed happily. However they were unable to hide their unease about Guddi's consideration. She has not met them for years."

They reached the hotel. Sanjay parked the car and handed a letter to Raju.

"They don't know about your feelings. What you are doing is a very big thing for them. Happily they have agreed to you, but there is a hope of getting back their lost daughter as well," said Sanjay. "When you meet her, hand this letter to her. Her parents have sent it."

Raju held the letter, his one foot on the ground and other in the car. "I'm afraid, Bhaiji. Every time I run away from her, life drags me back just to give me a heartbreak. And every time, the pain is more intense than the previous time. I'm afraid of what time has in store for me this time."

"We got married in a temple and were happy to get married. For our living, we worked together at one small restaurant. Of course, the money was not enough, but we were making ends meet. One-and-a-half year passed and I gave birth to a baby girl. I was happy to be a parent but not him, and that I realized later when his behaviour changed with time. He became depressed as he had always wanted only one child, that too only a son.

"His love and care was replaced by hate and frustration. Sometimes, when he was drunk, he even raised his hand on me. But I tolerated all that because I loved him. And had Baby, that's what I call my daughter out of love, I would have survived like that, but the day he came drunk and abused Baby not been there, I realized his frustration was turning from me to Baby. I walked out of his life and began my own."

Guddi was sitting with Raju in the hotel restaurant. She had finally agreed to speak to him after consistent requests.

She looked beautiful – radiating an abundance of happiness and peace. And her eyes, those piercing black eyes, were killer! She continued to look at Raju, and then after a long silence, she told him the story of her own experience.

Guddi had fallen in love with Keshav in the first year of college. He was her closest friend. Soon they got romantically involved. Her parents came to know about them and since

Keshav was from a different caste, her parents tried their best to keep them away from each other. She didn't want to lose her first and last love. But she knew her parents would have never let them stay together. Resultantly, she ran away with him and they came to Delhi. They got happily married. But once Baby came into their lives, a distance was created between them. They separated.

She felt betrayed. She had just failed in every aspect and become a loser. She had gotten the title of a prostitute from him. She still loved him and did not care for her self-respect. She lived with his memories till she learnt that he had remarried and fathered son. Guddi cried bitterly that day as she had lost him forever, but since she herself had been the one to choose that path, she had to bear the consequences.

"Once I saw my grandfather forcing himself on my mother. I was in the first standard right then and couldn't understand what was happening. But as I grew up, I saw them together a number of times, and I realized something wrong was happening. Being a woman, I hated my grandfather. I felt bad for my mother for having had to bear such injustices over the years.

"When I told Keshav this, he said, 'It's happening for almost two decades, why doesn't your mother raise her voice and tell your father? Why has she been silent since then?'

"I had no answers to his questions, and later when we fought, he brought up my mother's character and me. And my mother was not the only victim in my family! After I ran away with Keshav, one of my cousins came to meet me a few years later. By then, Keshav and I had separated. My cousin too physically assaulted me. I was a damned woman. I knew this society would curse me and put the blame on me, because I had run away, because I had married someone from a different caste, and because I had given birth to a daughter."

Raju looked stunned. He frowned. He was shocked by her incredible transformation. Gone was the chubbiness and bubbliness. Instead, the woman in front of him appeared to be sad and serious. Her eyes, though beautiful, seemed dull and weighed down with heavy sorrows. She was no longer radiating an abundance of vitality and energy. Instead, she had become the half alive body into which breaths had been forced.

"My life had lost all purpose. Perhaps the saddest thing had happened to me. Really, one of the worst things about bad times is the restless mind filled with questions, questions, and questions! A state of strange confusion. At times you feel stuck. I was really tired faking it to the world. Faking a smile with pain in the heart is so difficult! My friends named me smiley as they never saw me crying. Obviously my tears were only felt by my pillow and the sound of my weeping was lost in the silence of dark nights. They call me 'best-friend-material' as they could always count on me. But little did they know it was because I knew the pain of standing alone. I wanted to hate him for not loving me back in the way I did, but at the same time I loved him even more. One's first love always resides in one's heart, I think. Memories are unforgettable. The first time when he had held my hand, I wished that he'd hold it forever. I wish he would at least realize one day, that love does not mean physical attraction and sex. Man has been using woman for his physical needs for ages in the name of love, and I'm pretty sure it will continue for ages. I wish this race of humankind realizes how wonderful a feeling love is, and that there's so much more to it. It's a feeling beyond words, true that!"

That day Raju saw the other side of the coin. Once love and marriage had been a joke for Guddi. But time had changed her, and shown her the truth of life. Not only he, but she too had gone through pain. Immense pain! And because of that pain she understood the essence of pure relations. She too believed in love and its power, though her life had many questions unanswered.

Guddi added, "The day I got to know about your success at the hotel, I have no words to express how good I felt to see you. While watching you when you were standing on the stage, I felt as if I had no regrets, especially at that time when you were presented with a trophy."

Raju looked into her eyes. She continued to speak, and spoke about everything that had accumulated in her heart for years.

"My renaissance also instilled one more belief in me that all men are the same. But your renaissance made me realize that all men are not the same. There are a few men who actually understand the meaning of love and loyalty," she said. "I must say that you are a very strong man. I also wanted to overcome my problems once, but whenever I tried to do it, his memories made me weak. Rightly said, love is the best thing that happens to one ever, but I must say, it hurts a lot as well."

Raju looked at Guddi, expressionless.

"Guddi! So much happened to you and I didn't know it. I don't believe it! Why didn't you try to get in touch with me?" he murmured, after listening patiently to Guddi for a long time.

Guddi lowered her eyes and looked down. She lowered her head as well and remained quiet. He approached for her hand cautiously and placed his hand on hers while she sat still and silent. Her hand didn't move to resist, her lips didn't move to stop him, and her breath stopped for a while. He could say nothing as he held Guddi's shivering hand. He clutched her hand tighter to display his love and support. Guddi lifted her eyes and gazed at him. Though he had been hurt by Guddi, his eyes revealed a lot of love for her. They were magical and were so penetrating that Guddi had to look away. She felt a strong force hauling her to him. She withdrew her hand.

"That has been the problem, Guddi…you never gave me a chance! We were good friends once, Guddi. And you always knew that no matter what I was like to the world, I was always good to you. Don't you remember the times at school?" he asked.

"I do. But I knew you loved me. So I thought being away was better. And the fact is that I really had no guts to face you after knowing what you had to go through because of me. Especially after getting to know what Keshav had done. I never knew anything about those letters he sent to you to play with your feelings. I became aware of them after we broke up, and I was shocked."

She sighed. "Keshav is the same person you saw with me at the college entrance, the first time you came to see me in the college campus. It was the same day when you saw me after a year and the day you were looking at me with strained and eager eyes in astonishment, when my pen and notepad had fallen down. And later at the falls, he was the one about whom I had told you."

A smile came on his face thinking she remembered all the details about their meeting in her college.

She added, "You accept it or not, but there's a big role I've played in ruining you."

He raised his eyebrows. "In ruining me? Correct your words, dear. What I was or what I would have been? But look, what I am! Of course, there's a big role you played, but in creating me."

"Everyone likes the beauty of a butterfly, but none acknowledges the stages it goes through to turn into such a heart winning creation," said Guddi. "What would you have done?"

Guddi turned mournful. Her voice and expression changed. And as a change came upon her, the moon started to rise, the birds started to empty the surroundings, the color of the sky turned orange, and sun started to turn red, half hidden behind clouds, portraying the shape of heart and signifying the essence of love. The evening had arrived.

He looked into her eyes. She looked down. He continued to gaze into them. Soon she lifted her eyelids. He was still looking at her. A chill went through her body.

"Marry me Guddi!" Raju said abruptly.

A chill went through her body once again. "What?" Guddi almost shouted.

She was taken by surprise. The world considers the lover an emotional fool, but he is the most practical fox in the universe. He never eyes on his love with doubt or suspicion, even though he loses everything for just being in love with that person. He knows where his love lies, and where his peace. Raju was one among a very few of such a kind. His feelings for Guddi were purer than the Ganga and more eternal than eternity itself.

"Yes Guddi. You're alone and so am I. And above all, I love you, and have always loved you…since forever. We'll make a very good couple. Trust me dear, I won't hurt you ever." He was persistent.

"No," she said, "This is not right. In fact, we should not even talk of such things. Please!"

"Guddi, not for me, not for my feelings, not for that everlasting and immortal love I have for you, but for your baby. And a baby needs the love of not only a mother, but a father too. I'll be a good dad."

He was not crying. Nor did he seem emotional. But his eyes had a spark, and he was persistent. Persistent like a child.

"Please! What will people say?" Guddi found herself helpless.

"I don't care. I have not loved you for them, nor do I do it now. I have always loved you for myself. And who people? Those who rejected you, or the ones whom you rejected? Let's not ruin ourselves further because of them. Please."

Guddi looked around. In a beautiful restaurant were beautiful ladies accompanied by handsome men. In the background was melodious live instrumental music being played by a few musicians. On every table were small vases with red roses in them. A few couples had started feeding each other and a few had even started dancing. The light had turned dim, and Raju's eyes were emitting rays of love and lighting the surroundings with romance. Not only was he trying to win Guddi, but making the mood for all the lovers. His one pure heart was spreading the vibes of love to everyone around.

"Your parents have agreed to our marriage, Guddi, if it helps in convincing you," he added.

"You met them?" Guddi asked shocked.

"Sanjay Bhaiji went with my father with a marriage proposal for us. They agreed. They were angry with you once. But they miss you. Let's all reunite," said Raju.

Guddi's eyes became moist at the mention of her parents. She had lost them for a bad future.

"I had given myself to someone else, Raju. I never loved you, and I don't love you now. I cheated my parents and ruined my life. I cannot ruin your life." Guddi cried.

"Who says you'll ruin me? And who says you should always marry a person you love? My grandparents never loved each other before their marriage, nor did my parents, still they lived a happy life. I am not expecting a love marriage Guddi. All I am asking you for is an arranged marriage, because I'm sure one day you'll love me," he said.

Eager to spend his remaining life with Guddi, loving her and supporting her, to attain the peace of body and soul, Raju tried his best to convince her. Guddi had become more than his love for him. He felt she was his responsibility and that he was responsible for her happiness.

"And what if I'll not?" asked Guddi.

"I know you will. I hope at least now, unlike schooldays, you have realized that there's so much more to love and marriage," he said, smiling. "Don't even think of what you've left behind. Never!"

"Why do you love me like this?" Guddi asked, turning half frustrated.

She had asked an inappropriate question to which he didn't have the answer. All he knew was he had loved her, and had dreamt of a future for them. He wrote letters, and had fallen more deeply in love with her. He had cheated people, and had become a rich man. He loved her because every time he ran away from her, his other half, her soul, hauled him back.

"Guddi, my dear, I have accomplished so much in life. I have a good job, I have three cars, I have good money and I have my family with me. Here, in this country, I am a prosperous man. But I am incomplete, Guddi. I have always been incomplete! I lived in frustration. But the day I saw you at the hotel, I realized all I need is you. Only you can make me complete."

All a young man needs is a young woman to love and be loved, Usha had said. Where our heart is, there lies peace for us, and his heart was with Guddi. His peace was in her.

His childishness had disappeared. For the first time during the conversation Raju turned serious, and his eyes reflected deep love for Guddi.

"Life is about everything, but without love it's nothing." He said, "Till today I had loved you with longing, but from now on I'll love you with hope."

"Few years ago, I ran away with someone, and then few years later, he with his responsibilities. I became pregnant. He fought, and he left. I was not considered a woman, but rubbish. I was dumped in a bin of pain and sorrow. And you say you want to marry me and spend your entire life with me. How could you?" Guddi's voice was shrill and her eyes moist.

Now, being a woman, two things Guddi had always wanted more than money and sex were love and respect. And she had always remained deprived of the two. She had the opportunity now, and she knew he'd always love her. But still, there was a hint of uncertainty. She had had enough in her life. She was not in favour of taking chances now, that too when Baby's life was at stake. It's true that for a woman, her honour is the greatest and most valuable trinket she possesses, but, in the avatar of a mother, her child is a woman's greatest and most valuable asset.

"I'm sorry Guddi. I understand that any pain you feel will never compare to the regret you'll feel when walking away from your love. But you've really misjudged my feelings for you. If you think even I'll do the same, then you are wrong. And if you think after knowing this my feelings for you have changed even a bit, then you are absolutely wrong," he said, and stood to leave.

Raju was doubted and his love was questioned without words. He had lost once more! He paid the bill and left.

And just as he had left rejected and lost, Guddi noticed the romance in the air ending and people leaving from the restaurant. The love in the air had diminished and the melodious romantic music had ceased. Not even stars were out that evening, and the sky was covered with dark black clouds.

Guddi saw the letter and sat there motionless. She couldn't believe the one she doubted and had hurt the most had given his everything to her. She was hauled back to her pain she was trying to run away from since years. Her head rested on her palms, her elbows on the table as she sat alone. She had rejected a man who had loved her always, a lover who was born to love her, and a lover who was born to die loving her. It had been years that something good had arrived at her doorstep. Those few minutes were the most conflicting ones of her life. All at once she felt loved, wanted, cared for, and yes, even respected. He had changed her outlook on men. He had allowed her the opportunity to grasp and live a life with laughter, excitement and fulfillment that every human dreams of. But, she had rejected him!

Finally, after trying hard and losing against his only love, he, the villager-turned-millionaire had left, and walked out of the restaurant into the darkness of the city. As she sat alone and collected her thoughts, she noticed something on the table. It was an envelope – the letter from her parents and a bridge connecting the dark past and the bright future.

Guddi beta,

We know we are separated with a broad line. At that point in time you couldn't understand us and at a point we couldn't understand you. This is not a time to blame one another or to judge. All we want to tell you is that every parent loves their child the most. We have loved you always. If we didn't support one decision doesn't mean we don't love you. May be at eighteen you couldn't have understood, but we hope at twenty-five you do. You too are a mother now.

If you still think we were wrong when you wanted to come back, we are ready to apologize. We don't mind apologizing if we get our child back. The same way, you should never mind apologizing if one confession can make a loved one close to you. To return home is your decision, but if you ask us, come back and marry Raju.

Raju is a wonderful boy. His father is a wonderful person. His brother-like friend Sanjay is most reputed, someone with a big heart. They are people who want to make you the honour of their family, returning to you the respect a woman deserves. We have agreed to Raju, Guddi. Now it's your call. Hold his hand for good – for your own good, for your daughter's good. For everyone's good.

Come home. Give us one chance to send you off with respect. It was a dream since your birth.

With love,

Your loving parents

Guddi's eyes turned red as she read the letter and she broke into sobs. As she cried in the restaurant, torn and alone, she thought about the limitless love Raju had for her, and the love she had not even imagined in her dreams. She thought about how it might feel to be in love again, and about the feeling she had always been deprived of. Maybe, she too, one day, would fall in love with him. With all these considerations on her mind, she felt torn, because she had rejected what was nothing but utter happiness. People looked at her, but she didn't care. She cried even more. Just then, she felt a hand on her shoulder.

"Hi, the voices in my head told me to come and talk to you. Is it true that the three words guaranteed to humiliate men, everywhere, are 'hold my purse'?"

Standing next to her chair, was Raju. "I'm even ready to hold your purse, everywhere you go, dear. Even your shopping bags! I'll do whatever makes you smile, and then after many years, one day, you'll do something to make me smile. Trust me Guddi, I really love you. And I'll love Baby Priyanka more than myself. More than you! That's your...oh sorry...our daughter's name, right?" he was looking at Guddi, smiling, holding a red rose in one hand.

Guddi was dazed and looked at him gloomily, her eyes still wet.

"All said and done," said Raju.

He sat on his knees, and taking out a ring from his pocket he proposed,

Shivani Chauhan,
I give you this ring, wear it with love and joy.
I choose you to be my wife,
to have and to hold from this day forward
for better, for worse,
for richer, for poorer,
in sickness and in health,
to love and to cherish as long as we both shall live.
And hereto I pledge you my faithfulness.
Do you take me,
Rajendra Pratap Thakur,
to be your wedded husband?

He is such a crazy man, she thought and smiled. And then she nodded and finally accepted him:

Yes, I do!
I...
Shivani Chauhan,
take you
Rajendra Pratap Thakur,
to be my wedded husband.
To have and to hold from this day forward,
for better, for worse,
for richer, for poorer,
in sickness and in health,
to love and to cherish,
till death do us part.
And hereto I pledge you the same – my faithfulness.

She gave him her hand. He heaved a sigh of relief and slid the ring on her ring finger. From that day, it was Guddi that was most important, and not his work. He, our hero, Raju looked forward to her happiness every day, and tried to make the next day even better for her. He waited for the day when she'd embrace him by herself, and he waited for a day when he'd feel her love. From that day on, it were the three words that were important, and what he lived for.

Epilouge

One Year Later

Raju looks at Guddi. She is looking at him. Their eyes meet. They both smile.

Raju sits looking at the waterfall for a long time, remembering how years ago, at the same waterfalls, he had waited for Guddi. He remembers the day they had been there, and Guddi had left in a rage. He remembers the day in Delhi when he had proposed to her. And then he thinks of the journey, from the day when Guddi left in a rage to the day when he proposed to her in Delhi – a journey he had taken in order to pursue his dream to love. If he hadn't fallen in love with Guddi and hadn't believed in his love, he would have never met Sanjay, Sridevi, started his own company… and reunited families.

"What happened?" asks Guddi.

"We both had met here long ago. Remember the day?" asks Raju.

Guddi nods and smiles.

He continues, "I loved you so much even then. Why didn't you accept my love?"

"Had I done it then, your journey would have been incomplete. You wouldn't have gone to Bombay and become a prosperous man, a wise man," she answers, and prods, "and you wouldn't have met the beautiful Usha and Maya."

He smiles.

"Not more beautiful than you," he says shyly.

It had been a year since they got married. It was an arranged marriage, and soon after, they headed to London. A few months later Sanjay announced his marriage and there they were back in Dhaneri to attend the mating of their hearts. Sanjay, Madhav and Harish were happy to meet each other after a long while, and so was Raju, Guddi and their family.

It has been one year that they have been married, but they have not felt each other's touch. Guddi is never comfortable. Of course, he wants to feel her touch and her presence, but he can live without her touch, but not with the regret that he forced her to do something she didn't want. He is happy with Baby Priyanka as a daughter and gives her all the love and care a child deserves from her father.

The next day, as Guddi had told Madhav once, Guddi and Raju are heading to Switzerland for their first anniversary along with the newly-wedded couple Sanjay and his wife, to fulfill one of her many dreams. And like Harish had said, our hero doesn't have any plans to leave his lady love Guddi there and then go after twenty-five years to get her back. Instead, he has planned to go there every year with her, and come back together.

Before leaving for Switzerland, Guddi wanted to visit the place where he had proposed to her years ago, so there they are.

The place is still the same as it was years ago. He can still see the entire area for a kilometre, including the road that connects his village Harsi gaon to the other neighbouring villages. The rocks, bushes, trees, waterfalls and river are the same. Only Maa's dupatta is missing. It must have drifted away thousands of kilometres with the river.

The weather turns suddenly, and cold winds begin to blow. He takes off his overcoat, rushing towards Guddi, and puts it around her shoulders. He gives her a hand to help her come down from a rock she is sitting on, but she manages on her own, and he turns to head home.

"Listen," she says.

He stops, and he turns.

Guddi hugs Raju. His heart leaps.

He holds her back, and they embrace for the first time.

In her arms he feels a state of utter ecstasy.

"I was a dumped girl. Why did you accept me?" asks Guddi.

"Dear, a woman can fall for a thousand, and sleep with hundreds. But one woman completes one man only – a man whom she assists, a man whom she marries, a man whom she makes the father of her child and a man whom she holds forever. I am with you for the completeness you have given me," he says. "And above all, my love, I was born to do so. I was born to love you, in all circumstances."

The wind blows harder than ever, with all its strength. Trees start swaying with a great force and their leaves blow in the wind.

Guddi thanks him for understanding her and for giving her honour back to her.

"I want to become a woman from a girl. I want to become the mother of your child, and I want to make you the father of my child. I want to give birth to your child, my love," she says, and hugs him tight.

"What?" He is shocked and happy at the same time.

He hugs her even tighter out of love. Nature too joins the lovers in their celebration. The waterfall, his old friend, roars in delight. It sheds tears out of happiness in the form of the gushing water.

Guddi sobs, and finally says what Raju had been waiting to hear, "Yes Raju, I love you!"

Time seems to stop as their lips feel each other's touch for the very first time.

The things always happen that you really believe in,
and if not you,
then it is your belief in a thing that makes it happen.

Don't know for how many years he kept running here and there for peace, but he didn't get it anywhere. Because it was in Guddi's arms that he was to find it.

Today, his journey of years comes to an end, and life's divine reason is accomplished. Today, his heart is full of happiness, full of love, full of peace, and all of their manifestations. In his heart resides nothing, but only what he had always dreamt of – Love and Peace.

My heart is an ocean of deep secrets,
in which I want to dive in deep.